THE ANATOMY OF
LOVE AND MURDER

Borgo Press Books by GASTON DANVILLE

The Anatomy of Love and Murder: Psychoanalytical Fantasies

THE ANATOMY OF LOVE AND MURDER

PSYCHOANALYTICAL FANTASIES

GASTON DANVILLE

Edited and Translated by Brian Stableford

THE BORGO PRESS
MMXIII

CLASSICS OF
FANTASTIC LITERATURE
NUMBER FOURTEEN

THE ANATOMY OF LOVE AND MURDER

FIRST EDITION

Published by Wildside Press LLC

www.wildsidebooks.com

CONTENTS

INTRODUCTION

"Gaston Danville" was the pseudonym of Armand Blocq (1870-1933), the younger brother of Paul Blocq (1860-1896), a colleague of Jean-Martin Charcot at the Salpêtrière, who was the author of several books on neuropathology. Danville was also one of the principal collaborators involved with the early issues of a periodical founded in 1890 by Remy de Gourmont, Alfred Vallette, and others, which resurrected the name of a much earlier periodical, the *Mercure de France*, in order to provide a voice for the burgeoning Symbolist Movement. The new *Mercure* was not the only periodical that attempted to do that, but it was by far the most successful, and it survived long after the movement in question had lost its crusading zeal and Symbolism had melted into the general cultural background, eventually overtaken by Surrealism, which pushed a similar literary envelope considerably further.

At the time of the *Mercure*'s foundation, the Parisian literary scene was afflicted by fervent disputes between various literary "schools" and "movements," of which Symbolism was one of the most prominent, having developed out of Romanticism—once seen as revolutionary in its reaction against Classicism but long lapsed into a kind of orthodoxy—in close association with Decadence, a label resolutely adopted by some of the more radical Romantics, after having initially been leveled at the movement as a term of abuse by the Classicist critic Desiré Nisard, and resurrected in the 1880s as an assertive banner. Symbolism was widely seen as being engaged in a crucial rivalry with Naturalism, which was considered by many commentators to have recently evolved from its origins in the work of Émile Zola and the Goncourt brothers into a "neo-Naturalist" phase represented by "psychologists" such as Paul Bourget, the latter placing more emphasis on internal states of mind than external behavior in their supposedly-naturalistic accounts of the human predicament.

It is arguable that the apparent opposition between Symbolism and Naturalism was illusory, and had more to do with the fact that the Symbolist school was primarily a school of poetry, crucially associated with avant-gardist poets, such as Stéphane Mallarmé and Jean Moréas, whereas Naturalism was primarily a school of prose fiction, closely associated with the evolution of the narrative techniques of the novel. Naturalist novels did not, in fact, shun the employment of symbolism as a narrative device; nor did Symbolist writers, when they diversified into prose fiction, shun the devices developed by novelists in the interests of representational verisimilitude. Leading writers of both schools shared a keen interest in the seamier side of social life, and were routinely preoccupied with erotic and violent subject-matter. Nevertheless, many of the individuals caught up in the controversy did see themselves as being involved in an ideological conflict, and were often eager to take up positions in the front line, firing their critical weapons with reckless abandon. Gaston Danville was no exception to this general rule, but he was highly exceptional in the particular stance he took, and the location from which he elected to fight. He was, in a sense, the most ideologically-extreme of all the neo-Naturalists, but he took up his position at the very heart of the Symbolist movement, as a cuckoo in its most precious nest.

Alfred Vallette became the editor of the new *Mercure,* and his wife Marguerite, who had already become famous under the pseudonym of Rachilde, became one of its most frequent early contributors, along with Gourmont, Jules Renard and Saint-Pol Roux, all of whom would have identified themselves unhesitatingly as devoted Symbolists. The early issues established historical roots for the movement by reproducing various posthumous materials, including such quintessentially Decadent materials as previously-untranslated essays by Edgar Poe (French publishers never used the middle name posthumously grafted on to Poe's signature in America by his literary executor) and passages from Villiers de l'Isle Adam's *L'Ève future* that had been dropped from the final book edition. Essays and reviews took up the bulk of its pages, doing most of the donkey work in mapping out the field of

Symbolist literature and art and promoting its virtues; and while the page-count remained at its initial figure of 32, priority was given to poetry with regard to creative material. Once the number of pages had been doubled to 64 at the beginning of 1891, however, prose fiction was able to play a more important parallel role in carrying forward the ideals of the movement.

Much of the *Mercure*'s early prose fiction was very brief, set in the tradition of the "prose poetry" that had been launched forty years earlier by Aloysius Bertrand and Charles Baudelaire and subsequently hailed by Joris-Karl Huysmans as "the osmazome of literature." The crucial contributions to the magazine made in its first few years by Gourmont, Saint-Pol Roux and Renard all belonged to that lapidary tradition, and many of the other contributors followed suit, although, when Vallette was able to increase the page-count again, to 96 in 1893 and 128 in 1895, he was progressively able to find room for longer works, including serial novels—and when its periodicity eventually increased from monthly to fortnightly in 1905, those serial novels, in accordance with continuing changes in literary fashion, became a far more important feature. From the very beginning, however, Remy de Gourmont was interested in expanding the scope of prose-poetry beyond the merely lyrical, and adding more substance to it. In that quest, Gaston Danville must have seemed to Vallette to be a useful ally; his early contributions to the magazine resemble standard exercises in Symbolist prose-poetry, and the series he began to develop from them, collectively entitled "Contes d'Au-Delà" [Tales of the Beyond], seemed a natural development in terms of the elaboration of their narrative method and concern.

Vallette would have found out soon enough that Danville did not consider himself to be a Symbolist at all, but he obviously did not consider that to be a reason to exclude him from the periodical, the scope of which he was probably ambitious to broaden from the very start—and which did, indeed, ultimately become a magazine of general literary interest, as the Symbolist crusade in which cause it had been launched increasingly came to resemble a fad, and somewhat passé. At any rate, although Danville was never to appear as prolifically again as he did in 1891-2, he remained a regular contributor for more than thirty years; he published very little short fiction elsewhere, and the *Mercure* serialized three of his five novels.

In 1891-92 Danville published twelve "Contes d'Au-Delà" in the *Mercure*, plus two other prose-poems (the second and third items in the present collection) that did not appear under the rubric but can nevertheless be considered offshoots of the sequence; those items were reprinted in volume form by the periodical's press, with at least one additional story, in 1892, as *Contes d'Au-Delà*. In 1893 Danville published a longer story in the *Mercure*, which did not bear the same series title but is an obvious extrapolation of the same line of endeavor, and he published a further item of the same sort in 1894. After that, however, he changed direction markedly. He continued to write non-fiction for the periodical, much of it in a regular section headed "Psychologie," as well as serial novels, but only published one more short story, of a very different sort, during the Great War.

Danville's novels—*Les Infinis de la chair* [The Infinity of the Flesh] (1892), *Vers la mort* [Toward Death] (1897), *Les Reflets du miroir* [The Reflections in the Mirror] (1897), *L'Amour magicien* [Love the Magician] (1902), and *Le Parfum de volupté* [The Perfume of Sensuality] (1905)—all carry forward the same project that he had begun in the "Contes d'Au-Delà," as he explicitly stated in the preface to the first of them, which explained the theory behind the story series and advanced the claim that it would attempt to take the Naturalist cause to a new but logical extreme. The essay also identifies Symbolist and Decadent literature, in contrast to the various subspecies of Naturalism, as "degenerate." The essay is dated 1 November 1892 and is, therefore, contemporary with Max Nordau's scathing attack on *fin-de-siècle* "degeneracy," *Entartung* (1892; tr. as *Degeneration*), which Danville could not possibly have read before offering his own thesis, although he might well have had some prior inkling of Nordau's argument.

Vallette, who must have read that preface, although *Les Infinis de la chair* was published by Alphonse Lemerre, evidently did not take offence at the description of Symbolism as an essentially degenerate form of literature, but it probably did not endear Danville to some of his fellow contributors to the *Mercure*—even those who, like Remy de Gourmont, were perfectly willing to consider the adjective "decadent" as a compliment. Danville's novels do not appear to have enjoyed much success, however, and such celebrity as he still retains is almost entirely based on his non-fiction book *La Psychologie de l'amour* [The Psychology of Love] (1903), which went through numerous editions and was still in print when he died. He also wrote two other non-fiction books, *Magnétisme et spiritisme* (1908)[1] and *Le Mystère psychique* [The Mystery of Mind] (1915).

La Psychologie de l'amour was contemporary with Remy de Gourmont's *Physique de l'amour: Essai sur l'insinct sexuel* (tr. as *The Natural Philosophy of Love*), which was published by the *Mercure*'s press in the same year, and makes a very interesting comparison with Danville's book, given Gourmont's deep commitment to the Symbolist ideals and methods condemned as degenerate by Danville. It is not obvious, however, that the two books were written in an explicit spirit of rivalry, or, even if they were, that the rivalry was hostile rather than amiable. Danville's "Contes d'Au-Delà" were composed and published alongside some of the stories that Gourmont subsequently collected

---

1. The "magnetism" to which this title refers is, of course, "animal magnetism" as popularized by Anton Mesmer, and "*spiritisme*" is the standard French term for the notions usually lumped under the heading "spiritualism" in America and England; the French could not simply transcribe the American term because *spiritualisme* already had a distinct meaning in French, referring to theories of the mind that credited mentality to a non-material soul, as opposed to materialistic theories denying that anything exists except "matter in motion."

in *Histoires magiques* (1894) and the novella "Le Fantôme" (1893 in the *Mercure*; added to the former collection in the English translation entitled *Angels of Perversity*) and both series are illuminated by a comparison that suggests a certain mutual influence. The two writers did, however, follow markedly divergent paths after 1892, Gourmont remaining primarily preoccupied with literary matters, becoming the foremost critic of his era, while Danville progressively shed his literary interests in favor of concentrating on essays on psychological science and its sociological implications.

Danville was by no means the only litterateur active in the *fin de siècle* period to take a strong interest in parallel developments in psychological science, and the entire neo-Naturalist school, whose analyses of human behavior had progressed from the hereditary theses of Émile Zola's Rougon-Macquart series to the quasi-psychoanalytical theses developed with great fashionability and considerable commercial success by Paul Bourget, was more-or-les compelled to keep an sharp eye on its developments. On a more popular level, the rapid evolution of crime fiction had also taken aboard a powerful fascination with theories of criminal psychology. In Danville's view, however, the neo-Naturalists and writers of popular crime fiction were somewhat behind the times, routinely clinging, tacitly or explicitly, to scientific theses he considered to be obsolete. He wanted to take his place within— or perhaps to constitute in its entirety—a new *avant garde*, producing literary works explicitly based in up-to-date psychological theory. By virtue of that very fact, however—as illustrated by the juxtaposition of his most successful book with one of Remy de Gourmont's most extravagant enterprises—his plans brought the method and substance of his work into close association with some key Symbolist endeavors.

Because of its nature, Symbolist literature was intensely interested in fantastic material, and a good deal of Symbolist fiction is explicitly supernatural. The fact the Symbolist writers were operating in an age when supernatural notions had all-but-lost the warrant of belief, however—which is why Danville considered such traffic "degenerate" or "retrogressive"— meant that such motifs were very rarely represented as simple matters of fact; indeed, the whole point was that they were *symbols*, ideas essentially representative of something else, and not mere accidents of happenstance. For the Symbolists, the apparently supernatural was really the psychological, reflective of internal emotions and obsessions. Exactly the same was true for the Naturalists, the principal difference being that the Naturalists were usually up front abut declaring the seemingly-supernatural to be delusory or hallucinatory, while the Symbolists, not considering that to be a crucial issue, routinely left even the ambiguity unstated, allowing the images to speak for themselves. The effect of that distinction was, however, weakened—in Danville's work more than most—by the fact that Naturalistic narratives adopting the viewpoint of a deluded or hallucinating character are compelled to represent their delusions or hallucinations as *apparently* real.

The invocation of the supernatural in Symbolist prose fiction is much more obvious in short fiction than novels, and there is an obvious correlation between the length of Symbolist prose works and their usage of natural representation and narrative development. This is not surprising—indeed, it is inevitable, given the innate naturalism of the narrative techniques typical of the novel—and it is arguable that there is really no such thing as a Symbolist novel, the principal candidates for that designation being distinctly patchy, either because of their episodic quality (as, for instance, in Gustave Kahn's *Le Conte de l'or et silence*, tr. as *The Tale of Gold and Silence*) or because that they carefully embed significant Symbolist interludes in thoroughly naturalistic narratives (as, for instance, in André Beaunier's *L'Homme qui a perdu son moi*; tr. as *The Man Who Lost Himself*). That pattern is very obvious in Gourmont's work, and equally obvious in Danville's, with one notable difference consequent on the point made in the previous paragraph.

Many of Gourmont's short stories are "contes d'au-delà" in the perfectly straightforward and commonly-understood sense that they are blithely supernatural, even when their supernatural motifs are obviously symbolic of erotic urges. Many, therefore, consist of brief Gothic fantasies, either horror stories of the *conte cruel* variety or delicate dream-fantasies in a more sentimental vein. Danville's choice of "Contes d'Au-Delà" as a title for his own series was, however, consciously and determinedly ironic. The "Beyond" from which his tales come is only the supernatural world of ghosts and demons in the sense that images of that kind are held as a matter of ironclad faith to come from within rather than without, as products of the unconscious. Danville's characters are haunted— and how!—but they are very definitely haunted by memories and unconscious impulses, and the poignant emotions provoked by those internal spurs. All their apparitions are delusory, and although that does not prevent them from seeming real to deluded protagonists, in exactly the same way that the symbolic devices in Gourmont's stories seem real to his characters, the underlying rhetoric of their presentation is essentially different.

The fact that Danville was insistent in basing his accounts of delusion and obsession on what he took to be sound theories of positivistic psychology did not, of course, prevent him from writing horror stories or delicate erotic fantasies; indeed, it is arguable that it added an extra dimension of cruelty to his *contes cruels* and an extra dose of intensity to his eroticism. Although Gourmont, like Danville, was fascinated by the manner in which erotic impulses occasionally led to suicide and homicide, Danville's interest in delving into the psychology of suicide and murder is much more intently focused than Gourmont's. Danville, more than any other writer of his era, is a direct ancestor of his near-namesake Robert Bloch, the author of *Psycho*, and such post-*Psycho* extravaganzas as the works of Thomas Harris and twenty-first century television's extraordinarily elaborate exploration of *Criminal Minds*. His work is elementary by comparison, but that is the whole point of it: he was, indeed, consciously establishing elements and laying foundations.

In theoretical terms, naturally enough, Danville's work is unable to be any more sophisticated than the prevailing ideas of its era, and the psychologists on whose work it is based—primarily Théodule Ribot,[2] of whom Paul Blocq was a dedicated disciple—have long since fallen out of fashion. Danville's fiction is therefore bound to seem primitive to the modern reader in its use of the terminology of "hysteria" and its development of such recently-hatched notions as that of the "doubling" of the personality, but his stories were genuinely experimental in their day, not merely in their supposed scientific basis but their situation in the forefront of the literary *avant garde* of their era. The relative coolness of his contemporary reception

---

2. Théodule Ribot (1839-1916) was one of the great pioneers of "positivist" psychology, explicitly based on the philosophy of Auguste Comte, which eliminated from consideration all the nonmaterial attributes associated with the "spiritualist" school, whose notion of the soul had been philosophically revamped by Descartes, attempting instead to formulate an entirely physical notion of mentality. When Danville wrote his early fiction and essays, Ribot had not yet published his two books most relevant to their arguments, *L'Évolution des idées genérales* (1897; tr. as *The Evolution of General Ideas*) and *Essai sur l'imagination créatrice* (1900; tr. as *Essay on the Creative Imagination*), but Paul Blocq was undoubtedly acquainted with him, and Danville probably access to Ribot's ideas on the subject.

does not mean that his work was of no innate interest, and its unique features still recommend it for the attention it did not receive at the time.

The explicit connection that Danville tried to forge between literary endeavor and psychological science had, of course, been tacit since their origins and had inevitably become more obvious over time. The notion that literary depictions of human psychology, especially its more exotic manifestations, constitute a kind of research and analysis that can and ought to be considered a kind of *avant garde* of the science, perhaps far ahead of it in sophistication, had been proposed long before the 1890s, and the argument was viable long before the advent of the novel, perhaps extending all the way back to Homer. What was original about Danville was not so much his literary ambition—in which even the kindest commentator might be inclined to judge that he had failed—but his conviction that literature had recently lost its lead in the quest to generate understanding of human behavior and mentality, by virtue of maintaining overdue allegiance to obsolete models of motivation and the mind. Perhaps he had too much faith in the potential of contemporary psychology to correct that flaw, but he was surely not mistaken in his conviction that the literature of the future could and would benefit from further development of its scientific sophistication, especially in the artistry of its dealing with the human Beyond of the unconscious.

In the preface to *Les Infinis de la chair* Danville represents the "Contes d'Au-Delà" and that novel as one aspect of an endeavor whose parallel non-fictional development had already commenced in an article entitled "L'Amour est-il un état pathologique" [Is Love a Pathological State?], which was scheduled to appear in the *Revue philosophique* (edited by Théodule Ribot). It did, in fact, appear in the February 1893 issue of the periodical, and effectively constitutes a preliminary sketch of *La Psychologie de l'Amour*. The argument it presents is admirably detailed and elaborate, drawing on evolutionary theory (Darwin and Schopenhauer are cited) and literary evidence (including works by Paul Bourget and Benjamin Constant) as well as numerous treatises in psychology.

The article eventually refuses to conclude that amorous love is a kind of mental abnormality—more specifically, that it is a symptom of "degeneration"—in spite of its often obsessive character, but the conclusion is not without a certain ambivalence, and it is hardly borne out by the story-lines of Danville's novels, whose amorous heroes are all deeply troubled; the protagonists of *Les Infinis de la chair* and *Vers la Mort*—who are acquaintances—both end up committing suicide. In the context of *La Psychologie de l'Amour*, however, the most interesting of Danville's first triptych of novels is undoubtedly *Les Reflets du miroir*, which is an explicit extrapolation of the theory of amorous attraction set out therein. That too had a preliminary sketch of sorts in "Mousmé," the novelette included in the present collection, although the novelette is far more graphic in its hallucinatory imagery and the novel has a markedly different conclusion. The symbolic inclusions of hallucinatory fantasy in *L'Amour magicien* are more elaborate, but they are also more orthodox in their deployment of elements of Scandinavian mythology, and they strive for a simplicity that the preceding novel had almost seemed to be deliberately avoiding. That shift in tactics might have something to do with the fact that the *Revue philosophique* published a long and decidedly equivocal review of *La Pychologie de l'Amour* in 1895, by Georges Dumas, who alleged that Danville's "[literary] style is his greatest enemy."

It is, however, arguable that Danville's short fiction is considerably more interesting than his novels, partly because their necessary economy frees them from the tangled verbosity and ponderousness that often overtook him when he wrote at greater length, but partly, too, because they did retain, in spite of the author's convictions and rhetorical thrust, a strong Symbolist influence. The best of them retain a pungent hint of Remy de Gourmont, just as some as Gourmont's work—most notably "L'Automate" (tr. as "The Automaton")—retains more than a slight seasoning of Gaston Danville. On reading the "Contes d'Au-Delà" and their adjuncts as a series, it is difficult to avoid the suspicion that although Armand Blocq was consciously a positivist and a neo-Naturalist, "Gaston Danville" was unconsciously a Symbolist, and far more fearful of intimate hauntings that any true positivist would ever admit to being.

Danville's short stories were probably not widely

read at the time—the book version of *Contes d'Au-Delà* is exceedingly rare, and the early issues of the *Mercure* inevitably had a much more limited circulation than the later ones—but they were not without influence, on Jules Renard and Saint-Pol Roux as well as Remy de Gourmont, they and probably added some inspiration to the flood of *contes cruels* by such writers as Octave Mirbeau, Jules Richepin, Frédéric Boutet, and Edmond Haraucourt that increased its volume considerably in the 1890s and early 1900s, as the format was taken up as a regular weekly feature by several daily newspapers. Danville's stories are, at any rate, of considerable historical interest as foundation-stones of a dimension of literary concern that has never ceased to increase in its production and importance, and some interest has recently been shown in them by academics—most notably Nathalie Prince—and by aficionados of horror fiction (there is a previous translation of "Le Meurtrier" by Thomas Ligotti, which I have not seen.) Hopefully, the present collection will add to that revival of interest.

This collection includes translations of all the stories that Danville published in the *Mercure de France*, including the late and atypical addition to the set published in 1916, plus one extra story from the book version of *Contes d'Au-Delà* and the Preface from *Les Infinis de la chair*. With the one specified exception, the translations of the stories were made from the issues of the *Mercure de France* reproduced on the Bibliothèque Nationale's *gallica* website. "La Marguerite" (tr. as "The Daisy") appeared in the January 1891 issue; "Des Remembrances (État d'âme)" (tr. as "Remembrance (A State of Mind)" in February 1891; "En Bémol" (tr. as "Flat") in April 1891; "Le Meurtrier" (tr. as "The Murderer" in June 1891; "Le Substitut" (tr. as "The Deputy") in July 1891; "Les Illusoire caresses" (tr. as "Illusory Caresses") in August 1891; "Comment Jacques se suicida" (tr. as "How Jacques Committed Suicide") in October 1891; "La Pendule" (tr. as "The Clock") in November 1891; "À la derive" (tr. as "Adrift") in December 1891; "Lisbeth" in January 1892; "L'Ange noir" (tr. as "The Dark Angel") in March 1892; "La Rêve de la mort" (tr. as "The Dead Man's Dream") in May 1892; "La Lampe" (tr. as "The Lamp") in July 1892; "Vainement" (tr. as "In Vain") in September 1892; "Mousmé" in three parts in July, August and September 1893; "Le Coeur volé" (tr. as "The Stolen Heart") in February 1894; and "Le Cinq-Bras" (tr. as "The Cinq-Bras") in the 1 March 1916 issue. The translation of *"In anima vili"* was made from a reprint attached to an article on Danville by Nathalie Prince, available on-line at *etudes-touloises. com*. The translation of the Preface to *Les Infinis de la chair*, here entitled "The Evolution of Literature," was made from the London Library's copy of the edition published by Alphonse Lemerre in 1892.

THE DAISY

...A heavy, cold vapor envelops all the vague objects of the morning with its milky translucency. There are large trees, whose mute silhouettes loom up formlessly, motionless and somber, near the void of the road, like a neatly-aligned rank of tall black guards. Moving shadows occasionally appear, passing through the mist.

Dead leaves strew the ground with their tiny russet cadavers, and from the earth—the poor bare earth, stark naked, wrinkled by brown furrows—comes an inexpressible sadness, which rises up and up, invading everything with its bleak anguish, and muffling my soul with a melancholy fog of regrets....

Long streamers of white smoke flee. Pale phantoms are ungraspable dresses. They fly, brushing the treetops, sometimes torn apart by the branches, but without pausing, they fly, driven by a howling wind that chases them pitilessly. But now a more precise décor, scintillating with dew, is emerging from the ripped veils. Is the spell broken, putting an end to the fantastic appearances and causing the enchantment that kept sleeping nature in hiding to vanish?

In the east, a red sun tints the luminous clouds with blood, and diaphanous glints of opal; and, through a wound inflicted on the distant clouds, a patch of blue sky is perceptible, of that blue beyond aquamarine or turquoise.

Oh, bright awakenings, joyful awakenings, resplendent awakenings of warm summer, where are you?

Pretty little girls, blondes or brunettes, always beautiful; cheerful girls in bright dresses, who run around, chasing damsel-flies, beside streams in which nenuphar lilies flourish, where are you?

And you too, golden dreams, flamboyant with glimpsed ideals, blue spirals of blond cigarettes, roses blossoming by the roadside, lovers' kisses, shared intoxications....

Are they not among those which sometimes fly, before the implacable Hour, fleeing without respite in the sad Present, frail illusions so rapidly vanishing...?

That daisy! O poignant irony, contained in that spring flower, born there one winter's day—that dainty daisy, beginning to bloom!

...Yes, it was an identical daisy that I interrogated with Her.

Was it yesterday?

No, it was a long time ago; but I remember.

Now she's dead!

Oh, that little wild flower, how innocent and virginal it seemed! She too seemed purer to me than a lily.

Now, she's dead! Her eyes, her periwinkle-blue eyes...they will never open again, and never again, no, never again, will she drink my soul, with her lips with the mysterious caresses, her red lips, her warm lips.

How cold they must be now! But why is she returning like this, to my mind; I thought I had forgotten her. Yes, I can see her again, the frail and charming creature, who is no more....

One evening, when the stars were laughing in darkened skies, a warm spring evening, I met her—that daisy whose petals came apart in my fingers, strangely! Faint perfumes were rising from sleeping flowers. How beautiful she was! *A little....*

A little...a great deal...!

As she stripped the petals from the daisy, she laughed: a frank laughter that shook everything, uncovering her teeth, her adorable little teeth, as white as the white petals of a camellia. Her arched silhouette, outlined in the half-light of a clump of trees, in which only the thick tresses of her blonde hair gleamed, a gold nimbus, has remained precise enough in my wretched brain to trouble it still. Although very young, she had, at the same time as the mischievous charms of a gamine, the more depth of womanly delicacy.

Passionately...passionately...!

Certainly, it was passionately that I adored her. On seeing, sometimes, in the delicate oval of her virginal face, her violet eyes shining, with a moist gleam, my entire being quivered under the weight of an ineffable joy, and the marrow of my bones quaked with an obscure, vibrant and indefinable voluptuousness. She had made my life hers; and I believed, insanely, that that felicity could never end. I believed that, when the sweet-briar was blushing, the woods were draping themselves in emerald and the two of us were walking in the warm sunlight.

Now, the bushes are deflowered, the branches are weeping their leaves; it is cold, and I'm here, without her....

Hélène! Hélène!

Oh, the unforgettable, the horrible sensation! I'm not dreaming...my hands are moist with warm dew...as on that frightful night....

No, they're tears!

Why, why, does that memory always come back to distress me, like a terrible nightmare? It's true, they're not red, my hands...brutal hands...hands that have killed....

I had stayed up late that night. Bent over my table, working, the rhythmic noise of her breathing was audible through the door, which stood ajar. She was asleep.

Did I doze off? Undoubtedly; for, resuming possession of myself, as on emerging from a dream—oh, it was beginning, the dream, the lugubrious and all too real dream—I heard an abnormal sound in the room.

Was it at that moment that I had the atrocious idea of seizing a weapon? Why? But who can ever identify the obscure, secret, confused causes of irrational obedience, of blind, obliging submission to the orders of the Unconscious! Abruptly, I went in, and I saw a man, someone else, lying there beside her....

Still, even now, the vision obsesses me, with its disturbing and deadly precision. There she is...there... it's the pale brown shadow of her hair that casts golden rays in that manner over the lily-like flowering of her nacreous flesh, imperceptible tinted by the delicate azure network of veins, translucent veins....

They're here...in front of me...they're here...and they're laughing, I think....

Ah!

Have I raked the bed with my knife? I no longer remember. I have, it seems, fallen into an armchair, very weary, exhausted; and everything was red... red...the bed...my hands!

And while the cherished body became lukewarm beside me, a black slumber overwhelmed me.

I slept very well that night.

The next day, my eyes scarcely unsealed, the cadaver of my beloved appeared, alone; and I understood that I had been the victim of baleful heredity, and a deceptive hallucination.

Unless the guilty man...the other...has fled....

Cruel doubt, deep uncertainty...my reason totters; and...I don't know.

Oh, if only it were! No, I'm a wretch.

Hélène, Hélène, don't torture me thus with your accusing gaze. What reproachful eyes you're fixing upon me! Tell me—what ring of fire is gripping my temples?—that you forgive me.

Passionately...not at all!

Dear soul, you're truly beautiful thus. But...that

daisy is red…and what is that on your clothes? Blood! Blood…the sky is red too, and I can see patches of it dancing before my eyes.…

Oh, I'm suffering, I'm suffering!

My God…Hélène.…

REMEMBRANCE
(A STATE OF MIND)

Pale withered violets, whose white petals have closed again, sadly.

And before the faded bouquet she becomes pensive.

They had picked them together. Memories return to her of that spring day.

Beneath the nascent foliage they had gone forth. A perfumed warmth filled the forest with moist and soft caresses. The tall trees with mossy trunks were enveloped by sunlight, and bees were buzzing there. They had followed a path that opened before them, where verdant arches interlaced above their heads. They walked straight ahead over the most tender grass, toward distant golden mists. And there were flocks of little birds fleeing with a flutter of wings, flowering bushes that they brushed as they passed, ballets of midges humming in the warm air, and also carpets of anemones and lilies of the valley, undulating and quivering.

All those things made them happy, and they wandered, arm in arm, as if in a dream of love. He did not speak to her for fear of breaking the spell, but his eyes sometimes plunged into hers, informing her of ineffable adorations and extraordinary felicities. Her emotion was delightfully stirred by that exchange of glances, in which their souls sank into the infinity of contemplation. She would have liked to remain like that forever, lulled by the indistinct murmur, the continuous vibration, lost with her beloved in that isolation, in the heart of the protective forest. A vague languor invaded her entire being; she felt surges of confused desire burning her temples.

At the foot of an oak tree, garlanded with ivy, they sat down, and their lips met in a long kiss. Nearby, violets as white as lilies were bowing gracefully on their frail stems, and from florets with partly-opened corollas rose a fresh mist of odorous scents....

Oh, the pale withered violets, whose white petals have closed again, sadly.

Now the azure of the skies lights up again, and embalmed breaths of wind come through the open window. But the vision, radiant for her, darkens, because it renders the memories of the past more poignant.

She alone was in love, for her love was so strong that it forgives the ingrate the cowardice of the abandonment. But her wounded heart is still bleeding, and she cannot yet believe the hideous reality. Her suffering is renewed by the dolorous return of those moments, which she had believed to be eternal.

Daisies enamel the meadows; she will not interrogate them any more, the lying flowers that reply deceptively. Birds are singing, which seem to be mocking. Why has this spring come back, so similar to the other—and how odious it is! And further new springs will be reborn, without bringing back her vanished happiness!

Tears trickle from her lowered eyelids.

She allows those tears to flow, whose crystal prismatizes the horror of the at-present, and gradually, the dolor that is their cause vanishes. Her soul becomes serene again and recovers a benevolent calm. The oppression that gripped her with all its force of a clearly irreparable consciousness dissipates.

And, her eyelashes still moist, but with tranquil eyes, forgetful of the past, unconscious of the present, perhaps confident in the future, she gazes at all that remains to her of a love into which she had put her life—the faded bouquet—and smiles at the pale withered violets, whose white petals have closed again, sadly.

FLAT

Not the color, but nothing but the shade.
Oh, the shade alone betroths
The dream to the dream and the flute to the horn.

Paul Verlaine

I.

The feline courtesan, the lascivious courtesan with the strange eyes, whose green-gold irises promise unknown voluptuous pleasures, mysteriously gleaming beneath the light weave of half-lowered lashes: the beautiful courtesan with the red lips, gazes fixedly at the adolescent, who stammers, trembling, naïve and holy litanies of love.

In the boudoir hung with blue silk, with bright hues of aquamarine and sapphire, where, upon the fabric, silvery poppies flower, the faint remembrance of a strange, vanished perfume floats, of vaguely hieratic scents, delicately nuancing the agony of dying hyacinths, wilting in a crystal vase.

He is as blond as the wheat-fields that shimmer in the sunlight, as pink and diaphanous as the pink and diaphanous clouds that drift in the darkening but still luminous skies of autumn dusks. He has the beauty of all his youth, the pure and delicate harmony of his adolescent forms.

He begs.

II.

She smiles....

The pale courtesan, with the canephora hips, in the collapse of iridescent fabrics, the rutilance of red draperies bloodying her burnished bosom, allows the marvelous orient of her teeth to sparkle, whose cruel whiteness attracts. She lingers thus, mute, almost disdainful, although enigmatic, and above all, incomparably charming.

And he: "O Woman, wicked, insensitive and resistant to my prayers, I would like to hate you, for I love you—alas!—mortally...but one of your glaucous glances disarms me. Before your idol-like impassivity, I feel the wild desires of a brute beast; it seems to me that there would be a bitter and powerful joy in tearing apart your frail limbs, of shedding upon the satin of your flesh, a little of the ruby that is your blood; and, winding the multiple tresses of your resplendent hair around my wrist, dragging you over the warm carpet, half-naked, howling, martyrized by a slow agony, in which I would delight....

"But these crazed fits of anger are appeased by the mere sight of You. Oh, what black magic, what invisible spell causes me to hear your empty heart—your cold, implacable heart—speak, when your lying mouth is silent, and the scarlet silence of your lips seems to me to be a benevolent greeting? Can you not sense that I am suffering, then? And my God, from what tortures!"

Now, tears come
to his eyes....

III.

Which she wiped away piously,
with her rosy fingers....

With graceful movements, seeming flutterings of white wings, she caressed the swollen eyelids, which soon remained lowered, allowing themselves to be closed by the gentle soother. His features relaxed into a joyful smile; he put his hands together, listening, ecstatic.

"I love you," she said—and her voice passed through the embalmed air, softer than the murmurous and plaintive quivering breezes of summer evenings breezes through the tremulous willow—"I love you, understand that, cruel doubting child, I love you, oh, more than I can say....

"I would like to take you away, far from here, anywhere, to a land of dreams, with silvery horizons, where we would be happy. Alone. And the sunsets, like the sunrises, would see us ever beautiful, ever pure, loving one another. Far away, Old Age and Death would leave us alone, leaving us to Kisses. The nights would fill with perfumes; the harmonies of invisible breaths of wins, rustling in the branches, would float in their shadow. Then starry torches would light up in the heavens, like nuptial candles, pouring waves of light over us through radiant space...."

Sitting up straight, she spoke, transfigured by love, the pale courtesan with the red lips, the priestess of the ideal, whose profile, with the impeccable lines of a Greek marble, a ray of sunlight, slipping through the incompletely-drawn curtains, surrounded with a golden nimbus.

Beside her, a large lily drooped,
coming to the end of its life.

IV.

From the pure flower, a faint aroma emerged,
exhaled like the last sigh
of a virgin.

More sadly, then, with a heart-rending smile, she went on: "What I just said...foolish chimeras! You see, child, it's necessary not to love me. Perhaps you have saintly illusions in the utmost depths of your heart. You don't yet know Evil: you hope; you believe. I don't want you, one day, to have bad memories, to think: *She captured my soul. I had given it to her, naively and confidently. She, the exceedingly perverse, the exceed-ingly cruel, deceitful Woman, left me, after having wounded me dolorously, gyrating in the cold gusts of doubt, desperate, wandering aimlessly through life, cursing the deadly initiatrix...."*

Abruptly, he got up, reproaches in his eyes, and he closed her mouth with a kiss. In his rapid movement, he had broken the stem of the large lily, which fell, landing with a dull sound.

In the boudoir hung with blue silk, with bright hues of aquamarine and sapphire, where, upon the fabric, silvery poppies flower, the faint remembrance of a strange, vanished perfume floats, of vaguely hieratic scents....

THE MURDERER

*...A single atom emanated by me
produced the universe; and I still
remain entire in my self.*

The Bhagavad-Gita

"...What mysterious, invincible obsession did I obey in that moment of crisis? Under what compulsion was the crime committed? My memory tells me nothing—nothing at all—about that.

"I remember a state of prostration, in which I sensed myself descending limply into a vague and slothful abyss, with the apprehension of encountering some obstacle, which did not become manifest. Then there was black, complete, absolute, cruel loneliness. That lasted for a time that I cannot measure, during which, my palms moist, my eyes half-closed and my temples burning, I abandoned myself to the annihilating oppression.

"A reaction set in then, in the course of which my efforts, attempting to get a grip on myself, seemed, on the contrary, to aid my consciousness to disaggregate even further, to expand sideways, dividing my being into two distinct parts, existing simultaneously.

I sought in vain to emerge from the implausibility of that sensation; the duality of my self became more precise with every passing second.

"Abruptly, I opened my eyes. In front of them stood a human form, which I recognized, after some hesitation: it was Me!—the apparition of whom astounded me by the persistence of its clarity.

"Yes, it really was me, a self issued from myself, by that inexplicable and yet conscious projection, by virtue of a kind of objectification, which even now I can scarcely comprehend.

"And I was in a dark street in an unknown town. A thick fog veiled with its crêpe the tremulous flames of the streetlights, indecisive and unsteady. Houses extended, very irregularly, some large, others small, and their blackened masses appeared to me confusedly, like sleeping monsters.

"No one was about: no one.

"Some kind of cold rain was beginning to distribute swarms of fine droplets, putting a lacquer veneer on the deserted roadway, glimmering in the darkness. Shivering from head to toe, *I* was walking through a greasy mud, and absurdly, violently, an anger grew within me, frightfully, caused by the lugubrious aspect of the dismal landscape.

"I arrived in a state of exaggerated overexcitement, translated by a precipitate furious pace, beneath the sting of the icy downpour. The ground stuck to my shoes, weighing down my steps, further increasing the irrational fury that made me curse inert objects, being unable to attack absent people.

"Then I bumped into a shadow going past me. The impact made my entire being vibrate painfully. Blinded by the blood that suddenly rushed to my brain, which was drumming a staccato march in my arteries, full to bursting, I fell upon her precipitately, with a strident laugh that ripped through the silence like a fanfare.

"She uttered a hoarse cry of anguish, quickly stifled, for I gripped her by the throat, sinking my clenched, glad hands into that deliciously warm flesh. We fell to the ground together. I could not stop that insensate laughter, which shook my entire body, but I still held her in the mortal embrace.

"Soon, she was no longer moving. After a few spasms, her heels hammering the ground—and I also felt the burn of her fingernails on my face—she uttered an 'oh!' that dragged on for a long time…a very long time.…

"And I experienced an indescribable joy in feeling that body quivering beneath me. I could not take my hands away from that neck, which became lukewarm, already more flaccid. My heart was beating mightily in my dilated bosom, and it appeared to me that a conflagration was ablaze in my skull, under the incessant assault of increasing madness.

"I was still laughing.

"Finally, I got to my feet, staggering, and looked at her face, at the eyes widened by the final terror, in which the reflection of the supreme horror was gleaming: the face, in which I could see nothing but the eyes with the whiter sclerotics and the milky translucency of the teeth, striped by a black mass—doubtless the tongue. With a mechanical gesture, I rummaged in my pockets.

"A knife!

"Oh, I can still see that steel blade shining, in the fog, as I brandished it like a madman. It plunged without resistance into the inert mass, slashing it odiously. With a few voluptuous tremors, I plunged it, fuming, into the gaping entrails, mutilating the corpse, obedient to some unknown need for destruction.

"My arm, however, became weary, and I fled, leaving a pool of violet blood coagulating in the rain...."

"'What a frightful nightmare!' I said to myself, when I woke up, my entire body racked by an invincible fatigue and my head empty.

"Now, on reading, the other day, the story of the latest murder committed by Jack the Ripper, the unidentifiable murderer, my dream came back into my mind with a frightful precision.

"A terrible anguish gripped me, as I thought, as I remembered, the details of that deadly night: that it was on that day, at that hour, in that place, that I had killed that phantom, who was, perhaps, a real person... how can I tell?

"Isn't it the case, Monsieur, that all that is very strange, hardly plausible? But what terrifies me is thinking *that it might be true.*"

The stranger, without waiting for my reply, and having bowed to me very courteously, disappeared into the crowd.

THE DEPUTY

The chattering crowd was maintained some distance from the coaching entrance by two gendarmes. It was near noon and the sunlight, falling directly on the black mass formed by the assembly, was turning the wide-eyed, puffy and sweaty faces red. In the confused swarm, sometimes dominated by the gestures of forceful argument, the white patches of bonnets, the blue of blouses and the check of trousers seemed very bright. Fragments of conversation rose above the tumult of whispers, along with the shrill exclamations of women, whose echoes were faithfully repeated by ancient walls.

The narrow street of the little town, where a few yellow dandelions and clumps of chicory enlivened the monotony of the disjointed cobblestones, contrasted in its mossy and gray decay with the unusual animation that filled it with exuberance.

Opposite the dark maw of the porch, gently swaying mauve clusters of wisteria garlanded the crest of a wall corroded by greenish ulcers, from which the roughcast had disappeared a long time ago. The penetrating odor expanded its subtle effluvia insouciantly, embalming the hot air.

Suddenly, silence fell.

An exceedingly old landau, whose rusty springs creaked at every jolt, advanced to collect the representatives of the law who appeared under the arch, their eyelids blinking in the dazzle of the bright daylight.

They climbed in: first the prosecutor, a fat man with the pink face of a *bon viveur*, framed by vague graying side-whiskers, with a serious scowl that belied the remainder of his amiable physiognomy; then the deputy, a very young man feverishly kneading his handkerchief with his nervous hands. His sad and preoccupied attitude excited a surge of commiseration and pity among the people stationed there.

"Just think, Paty," said an old crone, lifting herself up to her neighbor's ear, "how cruel it must be for that chap, having to carrying out the investigation of the poor woman's death."

Paty raised her eyebrows and nodded her head, with a bitter smile on her lips.

When the clerk, with a napkin stuck to his left side, had climbed up the footstep, the Commissaire bowed, remaining with his agents, and the carriage moved off at the trot of two good horses, cleaving through the human tide, which drew aside very respectfully, with curious expressions.

After a little cough, prefatory to speech, the prosecutor was the first to speak, while the antique vehicle moved rapidly alongside a low wall overhung by thick shady chestnut-trees.

"Come on, my dear Mersol," he said, turning to the deputy, "you need to be more...more *manly*, damn it! I understand your distress, and its necessity...I even share it. You loved your wife, that's quite natural, but in confrontation with the crime...um, the man—which is to say, the husband—has to give way to the magistrate...." After a pause, he added: "No clues?"

The clerk repeated, vaguely: "No clues."

"And what renders the matter more obscure is that—as Monsieur le Commissaire said, and, furthermore, I'd immediately noticed the similarity of the two cases—we find here, once again, the same procedure as in the first crime, similarly committed in your home, Monsieur Mersol...."

The young man straightened up a little and looked at his interlocutor. "I carried out the investigation of the murder of my maid personally, Monsieur le Procureur, and believe that it has been correctly concluded—certainly, since the guilty party is to be tried...."

"The suspect, you mean? Well, it appears to me to result...um...it seems to me to be implied by my previous proposition that the vagabond in question might well not be the perpetrator of the murder of your servant, Louise Pertaut. It's not so much that he persists so firmly in his denials, as that the same instrument must have been used in both crimes. Now, the man was arrested a fortnight ago...."

"The affair is very complicated...."

"One could believe that a mysterious fatality were suspended over our house." He made a gesture of self satisfaction, and resumed immediately: "Nevertheless, I hope that we'll succeed in clarifying everything. Hmm! In my long career, I've certainly had occasion to encounter cases just as seemingly inexplicable...."

And the prosecutor told his companions—who were not hearing it for the first time—the story of a frightful murder, the perpetrator of which he had discovered, thanks to his incomparable sagacity.

The investigation was definitely making no progress. Not the slightest trace could be found of the audacious criminal whose misdeeds had troubled the peace of the Subprefecture.

Two murders committed one after the other, at an interval of several weeks, probably by the same individual, gave rise to serious anxiety. For, after the prosecutor's maid, who had been found one morning in her room, her head half-detached from her torso by a huge cut, it was Monsieur Mersol's own wife, presenting a similar injury.

The local inhabitants, so confident and placid before, had become anxious and terrified. Now, every evening, everyone was hermetically bolted into their dwellings. Implausible rumors were circulating, and the usual conjectures were making their progress.

Nothing, however, save for insignificant details, had been discovered that was of a nature to enlighten the magistrates. Even the newspapers had renounced the analysis of such a mysterious affair, limiting themselves to the clichés ordinarily employed in such cases and criticizing the law in the customary manner.

It was in vain that a renowned inspector had been sent from Paris to aid the discouraged police; he had found nothing more.

The meritorious policeman had just witnessed a new interrogation of the vagabond arrested on the occasion of the first murder. After the suspect had been taken back to his cell, the examining magistrate remained quite embarrassed, looking at his auxiliary with an anxious expression; the latter remained mute, and seemed utterly perplexed.

A sound of footsteps having resonated on the creaking staircase, the door opened, giving access to the deputy.

Immediately, he asked the two men, coldly: "Ab-so-lutely nothing?" Then, after they had shaken their heads, without waiting for a more detailed response, he continued, gradually becoming animated: "Well, Messieurs, I'll tell you myself…I'll tell you how these two crimes were committed. It's necessary that I tell you.…"

He sniggered, and went on: "It's just that I can see those bloody scenes, as if I had witnessed them. Look…the first.…it's eleven o'clock, isn't it? It's dark… Louise has just gone up to her room, and the door isn't closed…she's waiting for her lover…I can assure you, personally, that it's her love who killed her.…

"Barefoot, he climbs the creaky wooden stairs, slowly, avoiding making any noise. What if Madame Mersol were to hear! Look how he's slipping along the upstairs corridor…she lights a candle, cautiously.…

"That evening—are you listening?—that evening, as he tipped her back on the bed, kissing her, a sinister ray of moonlight pierced the black clouds, the funereal clouds, and its mournful light happened to strike the neck of the young woman, who laughed, her face in the shadow. That neck offered itself, livid, with a nacreous satiny shine, and its swollen veins marbled it with vague violet designs.

"Oh, the attractive snow of that neck, so pale!

"Then he had a ferocious desire to tint all that white with crimson. For often, very often, the *Idea* of crime had been implanted in him, imperiously, promising unknown felicities…the voluptuous *Idea* of crime, the destructive temptation—how many times had it presented itself thus, so that he was unable to expel it from his mind! And if he kept a razor constantly about his person, was it not because he believed that the platonic possession of that weapon would appease the monstrous obsession?

"But that time, it was too strong; he took the dangerous instrument, and, with a shudder of infinite pleasure that vibrated for a long time in the marrow of his bones, he plunged the blade in, so easily that he was astonished by the final resistance of the vertebrae.…

"A man who hasn't known the joy of killing can't know the extent to which he was breathless with pleasure when the blood spurted. The red liquor gushed forcefully at first, and in rhythmic pulses, out of the sliced carotids, coming to inundate the face, immediately pallid. Then, by gradual degrees, the double jet diminished in intensity, finally trickling in minuscule ruby droplets over the warm throat, thus clad with a splendid filigree on incarnadine velvet, rapidly deepening.

"No, in truth, you, to whom nothing similar has ever happened, can't imagine what ferocious and ecstatic transports ravished the murderer!

"The next day, he judged the action abominable, and doubted that he had committed it…a bizarre contradiction of the soul! Now, take note, I beg you, take attentive note of how vacillating his poor thought-processes were, which collided so crazily with one another, making a great din in his skull: sometimes they brought back exceedingly sweet memories— and had he not delightedly obeyed the injunction of the *Idea*, the alluring and despotic *Idea* of crime?— sometimes the thing reappeared as an anguishing and frightful nightmare, troubling his dreams.…

"Observe, therefore, the incoherence of all that; add to it the mental disarray that resulted from it, and you'll understand how the man was utterly devoid of strength, when, for a second time, the *Idea* came back, impulsively.…

"Then, no more hesitation; the murder was as soon conceived as executed: the occult demon that impelled his arm had too much power at its disposal; he didn't even think of resisting it.…

"Again, he delighted in contemplating the fuming cascade of scarlet, fringed with dark foam, pearling the alabaster of moist flesh with its auroral blaze. But when they were entirely cold, when the pupils, veiled by death, no longer held a gaze, the fever that was hammering in the murderer's temples fell silent; he wept...for a long time...and I swear to you that his tears were as sincere as my own!

"In fact, Monsieur le Juge, hand me, if you please, an arrest warrant, so that I can write the name of the murderer on it. I intend, assuredly, to write it myself."

With a hand that was trembling slightly, the deputy held out the piece of paper to the two men, and while they read:

ROGER MERSOL

the homicidal maniac, taking advantage of their stupor, hurled himself through the window on to the stones of the courtyard below.

ILLUSORY CARESSES

"Poor advisers are the hours of solitude and darkness, when the black moths come to burn their wings of darkness in the flames of Dream! I'm weary, oh, very weary, of stirring vainly, incessantly, the incoherent broth of memories that simmers within me, surging forth at the whim of unexpected, undesired associations, like some villainous fellow, of whose presence you had been unaware, emerging from the fog in front of you.

"Life? An exceedingly monotonous and sad succession of gray things, when not lit up by the blaze of sensual or ambitious desires. And then, even then, it's the forcible, brutal grip of reality, the cruel hand-to-hand battle with the enemy sensation that quickly wearies the initial impulse, avid for better and colliding with the insurmountable barrier of rapid, fatal disgust, against which it dies.

"The arms, extended with faith, with force, toward suspected unknowns, ideals, fall back even more discouraged, limp once again, incapable of recommencement, as soon as they have perceived the interminable withdrawal of the goal, which they take to be a chimera.

"Why, then, continue the series of necessary but futile actions, perpetuating the quest for the unrealizable, and knowing it—why? And suffering the contradictions of its nature, the inevitable impacts, losing oneself in rebellions that have no result? When it would be perfectly simply to descend without shocks, eyes closed, into the soothing calm of the only possible Nirvana: Nothingness! Because, resident in the soul, bruised but lucid, rational and fully conscious, is a minuscule and perfidious leaven of unhealthy curiosity, disappointed in advance, but which nevertheless persists: a need to see whether tomorrow will be similar to yesterday, to today, to every day. Everything tells me that it will be...perhaps.

"How often will the problem be posed, without arriving at a solution, and who will compromise in seeking the marvelous, the undiscoverable Edens, the radiant horizons of pure light and voluptuousness, never experienced? Edens fertile in enchantments, infinitely renewed in searching for them in fortuitous, temporary intoxications—immensely attractive, to be sure—whose only flaw is procuring too painful an awakening, too heavy a disillusionment, once they have dissipated.

"These voluntary hallucinations are, therefore, insufficient and injurious, for they favor the intrusion of melancholy and disgust, which await you at every exit—as if existence alone, without that, is insufficient.

"I'm not a skeptic, however, and would like to

believe. Believe…in what? Experience, acquired with birth, is an ancestral legacy that I cannot reject. Oh, to make a new skin, to revert to the primitive existence that does not lack the essential bases of belief, because the centuries have not destroyed them!

"For the sky is very bleak where the eternally drifting stars shine, the same ones at which the people of thirty centuries ago, or more, gazed…how do I know? And what I just said was proffered for the first time a long time ago—a very long time ago. Did it even exist that first time? A risible murmur is that of human speech, the infidel translator of thought.…

"Here comes the livid light of day, and I haven't slept a wink!"

…A diffuse gleam fills the room with a vague clarity. With a few last flickers, the candle-flame goes out; for a moment longer, the fuliginous wick remains red; then it is carbonized, and all light vanishes from the lamp.

His forehead slumped over the books that have distracted his insomnia, an extinct cigarette between his fingers, Jean, his eyes now closed, is drowsy. Only his frowning eyebrows, and a few feverish shifts of position, testify to the continuity of his obsessive preoccupation.

Now, it seems to him that he is far, far away, lost in the depths of an infinite obscurity. The faint chimes of a bell ring feebly in his ears, and also the sound of whispering voices, too low for him to grasp the meaning of words he can hardly hear. That sound draws nearer, is magnified; it is the formidable buzz of a vast vibrating bronze; then, without any apparent transition, it retreats to the limits of perception, becoming a faint, indistinct, very soft susurrus.

He tries to move; his limbs are flaccid, numb and disobedient. Resigning himself, he takes pleasure in making that condition last, which suspends him between unconsciousness and reason.

"Constraining oneself to the adoration of virtual images, evoked by oneself, without caring whether their presence—what's the point? With the acquired sum of sensations, it's sufficient to combine them cleverly; those sheaves of things once glimpsed, grouped in a variable fashion, at the whim of the inclinations of the moment, will take on an adequate appearance of truth, a projection of the will producing almost all their initial intensity. I could thus attain a maximum which, by itself, would confer tangibility, but the limit that separates me from them would be very uncertain and very thin. In sum, that's the ultimate experiment to be attempted; why not risk myself in that adventure, virginal of all exploration…?

"Boletta!"

In response to that appeal, a door opens, and in a flood of light that makes Jean's partly-raised eyebrows blink, a smiling brown-eyed, black-haired child appears on the threshold. The unusual dullness of her pale complexion is tempered by a transparent amber glaze, which, by heightening the flesh-tint, makes her large shadowy eyes seem more profound and gentler, the blood-red of her lips brighter and more attractive, and the nacreous gleam of her teeth, almost entirely uncovered, iridescent. Raising up her torso slightly, she advances, with a extreme grace, and her hands, whose pink fingernails are glistening, form two bright patches at her hips, against the dark cloth in which she is clad.

Like funereal drapery, a heavy, mute and crease-free curtain, silence has fallen again behind her. But soon, at a sign from Jean that she has understood, beneath those little fingers, which become animated—and with what life!—the cello strikes up.

The harmonies, evocative of the hallucinations so greatly desired, weep and sing, growl and sigh, flying around the gloomy room like a long—very long, interminable—procession of phantoms, ungraspable and rapidly disappearing.

"Those notes that are strung out so slowly, seem to me to emanate from the invisible, from exceedingly frail hands…and to stroke my brain.…

"Yes, within my skull I perceive their rapid friction, as gentle as two flower-petals falling. And with them, I fall too, myself.…

"An anguishing and delectable fall, into blackness, luminous blackness, perhaps roseate. I feel that a single movement—less than that—would stop me.…

"I don't want to do that…do you hear, Jean? It's necessary not to do that.…"

"I know that very well, very well…no, a veil prevents me from distinguishing…oh! That phrase, in which the flats bleed; repeat it again, Boletta....

"Now I can see more clearly....

"Yes, I know perfectly well where I've heard it before....

"Laurier-roses and lentisks trembling over the violet water...so calm...with amethyst flamboyances...sunlight...a white swan...marble balustrades...and then, too, clumps of hyacinths and daisies...exhaling the warm, penetrating odor of swooning corollas....

"On the terrace, she's singing in a soft voice....

"The yellow and red stripes of the cloth....

"Her adorable smile, and the promises of her black velvet eyes....

"Always, always, Boletta...oh, remain thus, remain forever thus, trembling evocation of what has been, imprecise and troubling apparition! Don't go! What would become of happiness then? And I passed by, so close to her that I might have touched her, but I passed by....

"Now...now...." He did not finish.

Boletta was on her knees in front of him, sobbing. Abruptly awakened, at first he had a surly expression, and imprecations rose to his lips—but before the little girl's tears, his anger melted away, and, picking her up, he kissed her on the forehead.

"*Cara mia*, it must be time for your lessons. Go and get ready; I'll go with you this morning...."

The girl went out, smiling, her eyelashes still moist.

Left alone, Jean folded his arms, and an enigmatic grin creased his mouth.

HOW JACQUES
COMMITTED SUICIDE

Nine o'clock.

...On seeing this page so white, free thus far of any soiling, preserved from degrading stains—oh, why does my soul not resemble it!—I almost felt remorse just now at bringing a sacrilegious pen to it, which will blacken it with a surplus of bitterness impossible to contain within myself. I feel that if I don't express these wicked thoughts, suddenly hatching out with the force that only Evil possesses, they will oppress me to such an extent that it would be necessary to shout them aloud in order to experience any relief from them. It is not permissible for me to oppose them, by reason of their increase, the observation of which fills me with anxiety. Perhaps, once cast on to these sheets, they will fade over time, like the ink that translates them.

And then again, if there are others in the world as unfortunate as I am, their sufferings might be lightened by the relation of mine: it consoles me slightly to think of the time when I shall no longer be alive, but when these words might resonate for them—and I love them already, those unknown individuals—an echo of their own heart, attenuating its din. It's so good not to be suffering alone....

I've just reread those lines and am astonished that I was able to write them. No, I don't want anyone to know; my malady is one of those that have to be kept secret. I have to hide this notebook. It would be better to burn it at the last moment. Wouldn't I be taken for a madman? As if I were not in possession of all my reason! Alas, for the torture that is racking me originates from there. I can see clearly—far too clearly, surely—into the dark recesses of my being and can distinguish the play of its slightest mechanisms, but what can be done against the force, foreign and yet intimate and irresistible, constraining me to reflect on things that I would prefer to banish forever from my intellect?

Mad! Assuredly, I'm not that. Does the oarsman drawn by a violent current toward the edge of an abyss lose all notion of danger and consciousness of his strength in consequence? The peril increases without his being able to extract himself from it; for a few more moments, he forces himself to struggle, and then, certain of his impotence, he abandons himself, without making any more vain attempts.

Thus, tormented by the idea that imposes itself with the vigor of the ineluctable, I'm still resisting, but I can already foresee the moment when, fatally, I will be obliged to carry out the action, in spite of myself.

I remember a tranquil autumn evening when I was very young. I have a picture here of the frail little boy that I was, and it seems to me that the child bears a considerable resemblance to me. My memory of that painful scene is very precise—the first one in which the invisible, occult demon that I bear within me, and which is now overwhelming me with its perverse sovereignty, became manifest.

I was amusing myself greatly watching the turbulent and capricious rain of brown leaves, and the different fashions in which the wind played with them. And I was also thinking that it was very annoying that my sister Lily was ill, because I hadn't been able to play with her during the month that she'd been in bed.

A wisp of straw was particularly diverting; it's painful—and strange, to say the least—that I remember so clearly; it rose up a little, performed a few pirouettes, and then fell back, only to begin again a few moments later, without ever changing its location, even by so much as a foot. That made me burst out laughing, and stamp my feet with joy. Then my governess came in. "Little Jacques," she said to me, "You mustn't be so cheerful; your sister is in Heaven now. God didn't want to leave her on earth any longer, and you'll never see her again."

I could already feel massive sobs piling up in my breast, quickly becoming heavier, and rising, rising into my throat, when, with a bound, I fled into the grounds, hurling myself into the densest of the leafless thickets, because—and I knew that it was horrible, and that I would suffer from it atrociously—crazy laughter, impossible to suppress, was emerging in noisy cascades from my taut lips, in spite of all my efforts and my genuine grief.

Yes, I can still hear it resonating in the bloody crepuscular agony, while the wind was howling in the branches and the dead leaves were rustling and rattling, like bones colliding.

I shiver in remembering those moments of anguish, and the sentiment of my impotence added to my sadness. It was because the sins of a vicious ancestry had fallen back on me; corrupted by it, the blood that was hammering in my temples, was surging through my arteries, too slowly or feverishly rapid…and I ran then, disarmed, into the black wall of fatality that will not allow itself to yield, of implacable heredity, the evil urges of which I cannot resist.

Oh, those who sleep now beneath the cypresses— and I envy them—those who have given me the fatal gift of life, how I would like to curse them! For is there any torture crueler than mine…of having to defend oneself against a constant obsession that haunts you, harasses you, going almost to the point of compulsion? The idea of suicide imposes itself upon me with such persistence that it will be a deliverance when I satisfy it.

Until now, however, my cowardly heart has fled before the accomplishment of the act, freely consented, desired, summoned at certain times with all the strength of my suffering being. And, more unfortunate than Dante's damned, I struggle, full of horror, within the unbreakable circle; death sometimes appears to me as a gentle liberator, sometimes a cruel enemy, but is always present in my mind, lying in wait there implacably; and my enfeebled will-power can no longer summon up sufficient energy to protect me from these ravages and procure me the benevolent repose of Lethe, from which one does not drink twice.

Unsteady and weak beneath the contradiction of this frightful situation, I retain just enough reason to obtain a bitter consciousness from it, without it permitting me to go on. I can't. My will is both disarmed against the thought that is besieging me—the frightful thought of suicide—and unable to accomplish it.

Sometimes, it seems to me that I'm suspended over a profound gulf. A frail thread—so frail that I believe it might break at any moment—leaves me swaying in the cold wind, which bring me fine droplets of spray emitted by some unseen nearby torrent. And I can hear, a long way away in the shadows, the black wave that will wrap the folds of its damp shroud around me. I am certainly bound to fall, but the fall that I expect and does not happen, the frightful instant that never arrives, but is always dreaded, in which my body will rebound from the rocks, the expectation, fills me with more terrors than the thing itself. The air breathed out in great gulps by my breathless lungs cannot succeed in refreshing my blood, which expires in an eternal fever in my shivering skull....

And yet the warm sun is so pleasant, when it appears in the morning, dissipating with the golden arrows of its rays the vile phantoms that wander abroad during the silent nocturnal hours! To live, assuredly, is sweet then, even though many so hopes, so many tender illusions, have fled....

To live! To communicate every day through all the senses with the marvelous ambiance of great Pan!

Eleven o'clock.

The clock sounds strange this evening. The vibrations of its chimes resound so fully: spadefuls of earth on a brazen coffin. God, how sad it is!

Songs rise to my lips, songs of farewell. I shall write until the end. It's said that it's manly to have courage. It's only a matter of possessing a little will-power. It has returned to me. Too late.

Now, there are red patches fluttering before my eyes and on the paper, like so many drops of blood or minuscule crimson florets. The man warned me that it would take a long time, but I'm not in pain. It's necessary not to wait too long, though, and I want to destroy these pages.

The fluttering scarlet moths are too numerous. I....

At that point, Jacques stopped writing.

THE CLOCK

"The clock was old Sèvres, delicately worked; pastorals unrolled the rural grace of their amours there. There were shepherdesses giving their hands to beribboned shepherds, faded landscapes, with grazing sheep and favors in their fleeces. In a blue enamel frame, the hours succeeded one another in pale white reflections, and the hands rotated, coiled like little serpents. They followed one another, the larger one in a great hurry, the little one always waiting for its bigger brother to pass, indifferent to the carillons that the other caused to sound.

"Oh, the pretty chimes it had! A sound that one imagined as pale green or pale pink, a delicate sound like a threaded needle passing through silk, putting a thin, very strict hem on the edge of an undulating drapery. It made one think, a little sadly, of the distant time when the Comtesse, in a dress with a low neckline, with powdered eyebrows, gave her hand to the Marquis, and danced a graceful minuet or pavane, granting him beneath her fan, a discreet accomplice, an affectionate rendezvous, of which the Comte would remain forever ignorant....

"And its monochrome field of golden brown, where such flowers grew, of which I know none more beautiful: musky lilacs from Spain or Persia, or somewhere else, freshly-opened roses in a mysterious garden—for similar ones can only be found in the Land of Dreams—blue irises like the troubling eyes of young women, pure violets, meadow narcissi, cornflowers, daisies; all of my favorite flowers, great lilies with limpid gazes, and poppies, blooming in scales and crescendos, with charming pastel hues.

"On the fronton, a delightful Cupid, with an expression of mischievous pleasure, and a little quiver on his shoulder, brandished the bow of desire. He was perched on very light clouds, ready to take flight; his pose even indicated that once the arrow was launched the child-god would immediately return to Cythera, to hold out his impish forehead to his mother's long kiss. His laughing eyes are sparkling, the string is now drawn. Love is about to claim one victim more...."

"It was still standing there, on that sideboard, yesterday.

"The wall-clock in the dining-room announced nine o'clock in its coarse voice. I expect the little old clock to repeat the nine strokes, high-pitched and crystalline: on...two...but the sweet music stopped at the eighth. *That's quite natural,* I said to *myself; it's slow*—and I carefully turned the slender golden hand—but when I looked at it, a few minutes later, I saw once again the open angle indicating *eight* o'clock.

"Quite astonished, I replaced the two hands in the

appropriate places. Then commenced the fantastic duel, in which I ended up being defeated.

"The clock didn't want to show any other time than eight o'clock.

"I was afraid; I looked at myself in a mirror; my face was odd, almost that of a stranger. Was I dreaming? A table bumped into me and the pain made me conscious of my wakeful state. Returning to the clock-face, where the two serpentine lines were obstinately fixed in the same indication, I recommenced the experiment; it was no more successful. As soon as my eyes ceased to be fixed on the pale blue circle, the strange phenomenon was reproduced.

"I picked up the until-then beloved object in an angry hand, and a thousand contradictory thoughts collided within me. I thought that it must be a hallucination that was obsessing me thus, and that I was about to regret my violence; then, confronted by the observation of the fact, the constancy of which exasperated me, blind and malevolent anger got the upper hand again. With an evil smile, I threw it into the fireplace, where a log fire was blazing.

"One supreme chime was heard, and then the porcelain shattered, with a sound like musket-fire…while, kneeling in front of the flames, I allowed, as a necessary release, warm tears to moisten my eyes.…"

ADRIFT

Holding the glass of champagne in her hand, in which she had just moistened her laughing lips. Lucy approved excitedly of Raymond Dutal's proposal.

"Oh yes," she said, turning her head toward the blue-green mantle of the water, rippled only by the luminous wakes of fleeting boats, "let's embark straight away, since it's so atrociously difficult to breathe here, in this stifling heat."

On the cleared tables of the restaurant, the lamps associated their warm orange glow with the moist white of the tablecloths, bringing out the pale gold, mauve or carmine in the half-full glasses abandoned there, and enlivened the green bellies of the bottles with flamboyant glitter. Further away, filtered, diffused and tinted light brown, all those gleams tended to fuse together and dissolve into an imprecise light that varnished the immobile shiny leaves of the chestnut-trees. Groups could be made out in which the bright red embers of cigars burned. On the island's cape, a bridge was detectable, solely indicated by an arch of shadow.

A hubbub of tumultuous conversations buzzed

confusedly, sometimes ripped by shrill feminine laughter, ringing out with the timbre of breaking glass.

Something akin to a murmurous and plaintive appeal rose up from the brown river, which ran along the water's edge in a continuous stream. Confused, multiple and almost ungraspable, voices streaked the silence and padded the mist; fresh voices, muffled in tone; the moist voices of scintillating waves lapping on the ashen bank, through the reeds, which rustled as they resisted the hasty assaults of the current, in a constant, harmonious and sonorous vibration; the phantasmal voices of soft breezes, warm breezes impregnated with odorous secrets confided to them by shuddering blooming corollas, breezes beneath which the leaves of the shore undulated, reminiscent of a velvety flock of nervous and supple animals stretching themselves.

On the banks, there was the play of pale fumes, gliding slowly over the earth. Bright mists unraveled like old, delicate silken scarves. Their opaque veils tore on the bushes, which they decorated with fictitious snowy fleeces. Further away, they extended the real perspective infinitely, masking the violet hayricks, the stripped and naked fields, and the trees, with a milky vapor that was dusted with mat white by the moonlight.

The embalming breath of recently-cut hay was attenuated by contact with an obscure scent: the reek of the marsh, mingled with the insipid perfume of water-lilies and the irritating odor of wild mint, which floated on the water on summer evenings.

Lying in the back of the rowing-boat, the young woman could hardly make out the face of the oarsman. Furthermore, they hardly spoke, both of them subject to the mysterious poetry of the heavy décor of darkness.

The flight of the boat continued, monotonously, veneering the bitumen of the waves with sparkling metallic flashes, and tiny globules of silver accompanying the regular plunges of the oars.

They often prolonged their charming nocturnal wanderings in that fashion, between the familiar banks, happy in that intimate isolation, lulled by the dreamlike flow, the mute accomplice of amorous reveries.

With rhythmic strokes, Dutal rowed tirelessly, imparting a steady velocity to the light boat.

Suddenly, with an abrupt movement, Lucy leaned forward.

"Raymond, Raymond," she said, with an expression of intense terror, "stop rowing…there…in front of us…a black gulf…stop…!"

Her voice revealed an atrocious dread, the penetrating terror of a redoubled imminent peril.

As the young man, turning round, perceived nothing but the familiar contours seen so many times before, he thought, confronted with that exclamation for which he could not see any reason, that it was a joke, and he began to laugh.

"Come on, we pass this way every day; nothing has changed!"

He picked up the oars again.

With a terrible accent of fear, however, and a convulsive tremor that strangled the words in her throat, she said: "Oh, I beg you…don't go any further…I assure you that there are rocks close by….where we're going… that will break us.…"

Raymond, not suspecting the sharpness of that emotion, not knowing that it was one of those attacks of panic devoid of an exterior cause, perhaps more frightening than if they had a source in reality, took it for a pretence. Shrugging his shoulders, he launched the boat forwards.

"You're crazy!"

Then, gripped by a tormenting oppression that drove her mad, Lucy threw herself out of the boat.

The night was dark; they did not find her body until the following day.

LISBETH

When the blonde young woman with the low-cut dress came forward to the edge of the stage there was a laudatory tumult from all sides, a long salvo of applause, pattering like a rainstorm peppering rooftops; canes struck the iron tables, where the saucers and tankards leapt up.

She bowed.

As soon as I saw her eyes through the mist, floating in the thick atmosphere—her unforgettable eyes, by virtue of which I recognized her—an irrepressible frisson of anguish vibrated along my nerves.

While she sang, and the audience listened attentively, I studied her at greater length, and my conviction was affirmed by that examination. Not very pretty, her face—a trifle bony, in fact, and very pale—the ceruse mask emphasizing its habitual lividity even more; but with a strange grandeur, the dark blue, almost black irises of her eyes gleaming with an unsustainable gaze in the middle of a vaguely blue-tinted sclerotic, seemed like two abysses of infinity dotting the perhaps-banal face: two gulfs gaping over an alluring unknown, toward which one felt oneself drawn involuntarily.

Ordinarily, the lashes imprinted them with a gilded shadow, veiling their glare, but when she raised her eyelids, they appeared., with that disquieting expression of fatality, initially surprising, and then imprinted with so much charm, such a languorous tenderness, that one forgot the unfavorable impression, surrendering entirely to the enchantment of their caress, drowning in a contemplation replete with ecstasy.

It was definitely her, and the shock that struck me in the heart could not leave me any doubt on that score.

Thrown into confusion by the sudden flux of memories, I left; the orchestra thundered with all its brass instruments, and the shrill trills of the mocking, woodwinds, rising above it, laughing sardonically, exasperated me with a stabling sensation.

Outside, I remember, there was not a breath of wind to agitate the meager plane-trees of the avenue. In the sky, like diamonds scattered in a casket lined with dark velvet, the stars were shining, and darkness spread its calm and benevolent serenity over the sleeping city, only rarely troubled by occasional pedestrians or the rumble of a belated carriage.

A carillon sounded an hour that I did not hear. In front of me loomed up the resurrection of the past, the lamentable and funereal past, the murderous past— and what a swell of thought growled confusedly at that bleak invocation!

Finally, hazard—how I blessed it that night!—put me in the presence of the Woman who, I was sure, without having any material proof of it, without even any clue that could encourage me in the belief, had, as a secret, still latent presentiment affirmed, played a definite part, and bore an intimate responsibility for the death of my poor Jean, who had been so dear to me. I had never encountered, among the crowd with whom one is obliged to rub shoulders, another soul similar to his. He had been—yes, I do not hesitate to affirm it now—my only friend, the only human being worthy of that name, so often lavished wantonly, prostituted many times over, on those with whom a temporary or accidental communal interest, a vague similarity of tastes, or identical aspirations, seem to unite you in some way.

While he was a lieutenant in the light infantry, Jean de Sancey had met Elisabeth, the girl with the mysterious eyes, in the little provincial town where he was garrisoned. Subsequently, she had been able—by means of what spells?—to inspire in him one of those passions that hold the entire being in a jealous and perpetual servitude.

Already, the unknown woman who thus took the best part of Jean away from me, stealing him from my affection, had inspired an instinctive sentiment of repulsion in me, to which were added vague thoughts of danger—which, alas, were realized only too soon. So, I had always refused to become more closely acquainted with the woman who had separated us in that fashion, and whom I considered as an enemy, when I learned one day that Sancey had killed himself, without there being any explanation for the unexpected suicide. The other had not been seen again.

That story, never forgotten, returned now, with an abundance of precise details that revived my grief and my hatred; and immediately, I made a resolution to do everything possible to discover the key to the enigma. Since the sphinx with the mute eyes had reappeared to me, I would be able to interrogate her and, if necessary, constrain her to yield her secret to me.

In the distance, the sea extended, streaming with light beneath the sparkling kiss of the moon. The placid and mute waves bathed the white strand with a feeble surf. A lighthouse, far away, bloodied the misty horizon with its red light. Phantoms of odors drifted in the warm air, but the foliage was scarcely stirring. Before the tranquil peace of the décor, the fever burning my temples abruptly fell away, and the consoling influence of the pale and beautiful things surrounding me soothed the bitterness of the initial violence. The night bandaged my wound with the delicate and obliging womanly hands.

One night, I obtained the favor of seeing her home. Oh, all the way to the threshold of her apartment, we only exchanged banal conventional remarks, and nothing—nothing at all—gave me any hint the scene that was about to unfold. While she lit the candles on the mantelpiece, she fixed me via the mirror—I was standing behind her—with an indecipherable stare, and, at that moment, I almost lost all consciousness of the surroundings, abandoning myself to that black and white reflection, the enormous circle of which suspended me in terrifying anguish, in the feverish expectation of an unsuspected future.

"Bonsoir, Monsieur de Rèce," she said. "You've come to talk to me about Jean, haven't you?" Then, softening the tone of her voice, she added: "I haven't forgotten the poor boy, I assure you."

As if in a cruel nightmare, I saw her take off her mantle and her hat; afterwards, a phantasmal smile fluttering over her bloodless lips, she raised her head, and fascinated me for the second time with her wide open eyes. It was impossible for me to turn mine away—oh, the frightful torture I endured!

Was I then, the victim of a frightful hallucination, or was I not rather the spectator of the drama whose memory she was evoking internally? I watched, terrified and impotent, the scene that I had been unable to divine, but which must, in reality, have occurred between *her* and *him*.

In the little room to which I had come so often, Jean, his brows furrowed, a malevolent crease barring his forehead with an unaccustomed wrinkle, was marching back and forth, with the haggard expression of a madman. Brief and unintelligible words were emerging from his pursed lips. Evidently, he was prey to the haunting obsession of some evil idea. Then she came in.

"Lisbeth," she said, in a low voice, his tone veiled, but pierced with an ill-contained anger, "do you know that what you're doing is vile.…"

"What's that, my friend?"

"It's futile to pretend. Lisbeth, when I met you, you were poor, an orphan, abandoned by everyone, and all by yourself. I vowed to you, that day, a love such that it was only through you that life was sweet to me, and you agreed to go with me. I gave myself entirely to you, without restrictions, making you the mistress of my soul as well as my body—oh, I'm not complaining; I've been entirely happy—but in return, and you freely agreed to the pact, I asked you for just one thing: to remain faithful to me no matter what might come.

"And that was, for me, as you know full well, an illusory oath, for I did not think, even for an instant, that you could be lying. In that love I had placed all my hopes, and also, alas, all my illusions; it had become for me the supreme refuge and the ultimate joy, beyond which there as nothing but oblivion…but you did not see it as anything but a momentary folly, a temporary caprice. Tell me, why have you done me so much harm? I have always been submissive and very affectionate toward you; I was eager to realize the slightest of your desires before you expressed them.…

"Was what I had dreamed of so impossible, then, and, my God, what have I done that you should punish me so cruelly? Just now, criminal ideas came to me; I would have liked to crush the two of you together, as one does with vipers that bite. I've seen you again… and I'm weeping.…

"Lisbeth…Lisbeth…one word, and I'll forgive you.…"

She tapped the floor nervously with her heel, and

said, pitilessly: "I don't understand, my poor friend, and if you're going to go on like this for much longer, I'll leave...."

"You shan't leave!" howled Sancey, in a hoarse voice. And he placed himself before the doorway, furiously.

She had lowered her veil, and came forward.

"Let me pass!"

"No!"

"Let me!" And she tried to reach past him and take hold of the doorknob—but he grabbed her wrists, and threw her down in an armchair.

She got up almost immediately, beside herself.

Holding on to the curtains in order not to fall over, staggering under the frightful combat in which his crazed ideas were engaging in his brain, he made a movement, extending his right hand, which encountered the butt of his service revolver in the panoply.

"Threats!" said Lisbeth, sniggering. "You wouldn't have the courage to kill me. Well, yes, I've deceived you, you hear...so fire, then, *coward!*"

That word made him turn red, as a bellows does a fire; he pressed the trigger, having turned the barrel toward his head.

When the blue smoke had dissipated in heavy spirals, undulating like a light fog in the room, Lisbeth saw the lieutenant's body lying there, his blonde moustache twisted in a final rictus, his hands clenched, with a little hole above his eye, which was gazing vaguely, already vitreous.

On the carpet, a thin trickle of blood was coagulating, making a red stain; the buttons of his uniform jacket were shining.…

A cold sweat bathed my temples. I seemed to see everything around me dancing, the eyes immeasurably dilated, while demonic laughter burst out in my ears. They were laughing, those eyes, in truth, they were laughing.…

I fainted.

When I came round, Lisbeth, with a bottle of smelling-salts in her hand and her eyelids lowered, asked me, ironically: "What's the matter with you, my dear? Such sensitivity! I was almost afraid.…"

The slut!

So, I knew what had happened, and my just desire for revenge had never been greater. But so invincible was the power of her gaze—her horrible gaze, which seemed to be reading my mind, and simultaneously dominating it—that she became my mistress.

Yes, I committed that sacrilege, that frightful profanation, and I tried in vain to escape the yoke, to recover my self-possession; her evil influence held me captive as securely as the heaviest chains—not that thoughts of rebellion did not come to me.

One night, I got up without making any noise—a spider spinning its web could not have done better. On a table, a pair of scissors was gleaming faintly. I took them, and slowly—very slowly, I assure you—without my footsteps sliding over the parquet being audible, I came back to the bedside, holding them open in my hand.

How my heart was beating at that moment, and what joy illuminated my features! Silently, I sniggered....

Finally, I was about to be able to break that infamous union, appease my remorse, chase away impious sensuality and find repose! Since her eyes, her magical eyes, her vampiric eyes, were all of her strength, a single thrust of that frail weapon, and it would all be over.

Leaning over the dangerous sleeping woman illuminated by the alabaster night-light, holding my breath, I was about to strike....

Damnation!

In the pale face, with an almost automatic movement, the waxen eyelids were raised, and, drinking my soul, pitiless suckers, the enamel eyes of the ghoul commanded; she extended her lips to me—the thin red ribbon of her lips, which burned me with a kiss that only the eternal victims of Hell ought to receive....

And that passion endured, endured, seeming not to want to end.

Another time, I contrived to pour a narcotic into her glass—poison repulsed me. She raised the glass, smiled at me satanically, and then put it down on the table so abruptly that the crystal broke and shattered.

Other attempts failed in the same way.

Meanwhile, that ignoble perpetual compromise and my unworthy weakness made me ashamed—but in her presence, all resolution disappeared within me, like a flock of clouds rapidly dispersed by the wind. Every day, I promised myself to break that vile bond; every night saw me lavishing my caresses on the terrible fascinatrix.

No, no, the tortures that I experienced then are not among those that can be imagined, and it is still a subject of astonishment for me to recall that time of extreme suffering and to see that I have survived it!

This is what happened.

Every evening, I waited at the exit from the public place in which she was singing. That time, firmly decided to accomplish the act, at any price, I had equipped myself with a hunting-knife; it was open in my pocket, and on the way I caressed the cold blade. I was very witty, very cheerful. She did not perceive anything; I avoided, moreover, meeting her gaze, for she would certainly have guessed everything that night, as she had always done before.

I recall the whole scene very well. I let her go in first, into the corridor, which was not lit at that time of night. Then, whistling a tally-ho, overflowing with delight, I slew the beast, with a firm hand, cutting her throat. She oscillated, without uttering a cry, her head almost separated from her body, and then fell forwards, with a dull thud. I heard the blood gushing from her arteries against the wall, and also the raucous sound of the air, vainly aspired by the breathless lungs, in a supreme effort.

Carefully, I wiped the blade, and the next day, very calmly, I left for America,

And now that I've told you everything, Father, decide whether you can absolve me....

THE DARK ANGEL

A flock of pink flamingoes traversed the capricious silvery clouds embroidered on the turquoise blue silk. Next to the exotic wall-hanging, a little Japanese skeleton slowly gyrated, hanging from a candelabrum by a slender thread that Pierre could not see from the divan where he was lying. Velvety and tremulous, the soft light of the candle, lit when he came home, was reflected in the two brilliants of his heavy shirt-front and ran sparkling streams of fluid gold over his frock-coat, in the lining of which a minuscule spring of heather had almost finished withering away. The palpitations of the flame died on the edge of the shadow in which the young man's face was placed.

Sitting in front of the fireplace on a scarlet cushion, in a grave, almost hieratic pose, his cat fixed the faint redness of the dying embers with her phosphorescent eyes: emerald crescents striated with jade. In the floating gloom, traversed by diffuse gleams, the fabric shade of a standard lamp overhung a broad lilac keyboard, heightened by bright sulfur-yellow.

Outside, the wind was playing a vibrant and lugubrious nocturnal symphony, entangled with long chromatic scales, inspiring with its furious breath the organ of grave chimneys, and, responding to the appeal of the plaintive harmony, sad, feeble, dolorous thoughts were evoked, and suffering too.

Pierre suddenly felt the return of the oppressive grip that had dug into his heart a little while ago, with the persistence of a terrifying clamp whose jaws were tightening relentlessly, without meeting.

Now, simultaneously, there is an intense, atrocious burning sensation in his breast, and a kind of slow tearing apart, fiber by fiber, of all his muscles. He dare not risk a movement lest he exasperate the horrible torture. At the same time, his head becomes extremely heavy, to which is added the continuous fulguration of sharp, multiple, vacillating points suddenly plunging into it, assailing him indefatigably with their slender bite. His face contracts, he is suffering, silently and motionlessly—except that his teeth are digging into the bloodless lividity of his lips, and his fingernails are scoring the palms of his clenched hands.

At times, rushes of blood run beneath his damp, shivering skin in torrid waves, inundating his face, invading his forehead and then the skull, mounting a furious assault, while the unbearable pulsation of the arteries in his temples is like a beaten gong sounding the charge. It seems to him that his head is full of swarming beasts, whose innumerable and trenchant mouths and crazed muzzles are digging into his brain. Is it not about to burst? He is obliged to put the opaque and bloodshot veil of lowered eyelids between himself and his surroundings, so much does the slightest luminous vibration reverberate dolorously in his bruised being, multiplied tenfold by the fatiguing tension of his exacerbated nerves, excessively irritable in this moment of supreme and infinite anguish.

Then the paroxysm of anxiety is followed by a relative wellbeing, with occasional rapid twinges, commemorative of the terrible past traversed, like the last lightning-flashes of an easing storm, furrowing a purer sky still striped with somber shreds of cloud. The fugitive recollection of the evening, spent without any menacing presage at Madame de Prézilles' house, is sketched in his darkened consciousness, where foul odors of stupor float: an insignificant soirée, garlanded by the usual young women and the customary cortege of black suits, without the slightest memorable incident taking place.

The weave of painful sensations thins out, tears, and finally disappears.

Pierre breathes deeply, stretches his limbs, as if liberated from a nasty nightmare, glad to be no longer perceiving anything disquieting. Emboldened by the tranquility of relaxed nerves and corporeal serenity, he stands up, heads for an item of furniture with curious incrustations of malachite and jasper, and opens a drawer; it contains letters. He closes it gently, and finds the tobacco he was looking for on top. Meticulously, he rolls a cigarette between fingers that are still trembling.

Capricious arabesques form and break up, glittering milky blue spirals, rising up and fading away in a shifting design, stairways of candid dreams set in the sky. Pierre listens to the gusts of wind, the vibrant course of which is continuing. The racket is attenuated by the lowered blinds, the window-panes, around which the lead fittings snake irregularly, and the brown, rigid curtains, half-veiling the window with their copper-studded armor, the gaps of which take on a warm silky gleam of shiny new brass. The noise of the squall thus becomes a song, intoning distant melancholies, very softly, seemingly repeating the plaint of the waves on evenings when the tide is ebbing; and the feeble, excessively sad melody embroiders growling arpeggios over the monotonous purring of the drowsy feline, the gray furry ball of which is a palely-colored blot on the crimson satin on which it sketches an imprecise eclipse. The creaking of the dry woodwork forms sonorous breaches streaking the demi-silence.

Exhausted, not by the benevolent lassitude that summons sleep but by the arrival of discouragement, and the fear experienced upon emergence from danger, overwhelmed by the dismal and unstable host of ideas that are troubling him, the young man cannot make up his mind to go to bed, because he is all too familiar with the cruel insomnia in which agitated limbs refuse repose, the eyes wander in the darkness and the mind roams in the phantasmal night. Insidiously and perfidiously, however, a somnolent torpor numbs him, from which he tries to escape, fearing the advent of imaginary and terrifying visions, which bring dread, suffocation, intimidation and annihilation, with regard to a peril that is vain and derisory but nevertheless as dangerous as a real peril, and perhaps more so.

The lax and uncertain reverie retreats, fleeing through the free spaces of the vast field of memory and swerving into abrupt detours of association, which spur him along multiple pathways. At first he encounters insignificances, quickly neglected; then the landscape of fiction is animated, populated with characters, which take on a posthumous life; shadows, strayed from the utmost depths of memory, return to the light.

A face is finally detached from confused groups and divergent coexistences; black hair, nacreous shoulders of an ideal curvature and the tapering torso of a woman complete it. What caused that? Ah! The letters discovered just now! Pierre moves his lips involuntarily, from which a name emerges; then, without being aware of it, he pronounces incoherent words in a low voice, not hearing the words that translate, unconsciously, his intimate thoughts.

"She *must* be dead...I *sense* that's she's dead.... When? That night, perhaps! Ah, the strange presentiment: my bones are icy....

"How come that absurd idea has struck me, and at the present moment, when, by a singular coincidence—very singular, to be sure—her image haunts me, as clear in form as on the first day of her apparition, when, in moments of intoxication, she penetrated soundlessly into this room?

"Why shouldn't she be dead? I can see her now, so pale; too pale for a living person. In particular, I don't like the dull, colorless hair that masks the nape of her neck; she had such beautiful hair.

"Eh? Someone just spoke, here, and *something* cold and fluid has come in...yes, *something*...that cat has woken up and is miaowing, sniffling, her hair bristling. Truly, something abnormal is happening: what?

"I don't observe anything...nothing at all....

"No noise. And I haven't been drinking ether![3]

"The supernatural force of this funereal conviction frightens me. I don't *want* to believe in this glacial revelation, suddenly surging forth, unmotivated; but it's impossible to withdraw myself from the strange evidence with which it's overwhelming me.

"In winter, the daylight is belated in its appearance; the hours only take flight heavily, and I'm alone, alone, always alone without any other company than that of evil thoughts! So, was I not cruel, cowardly and pitiless when the stupid voice of pride spoke within me? I let her go, nearly ten months ago now...oh, after a futile scene that I could have terminated with a single word. That word was burning my lips; out of imbecile vanity, stupid self-esteem, I didn't pronounce it. With one kiss, one gesture, I could have retained her; she was so good, so charitable to my easily-wounded soul. My arms, which I ought to have held out, remained

---

3. Danville's story series antedates the series of tales of hallucinatory hauntings that Jean Lorrain entitled "Contes d'un buveur d'éther" [Tales of an Ether-Drinker] (tr. in *Nightmares of an Ether-Drinker*), but Lorrain was a close friend of Rachilde, and Danville probably met him at the salon hosted by the Vallettes—in which case he would doubtless have taken a strong interest in Lorrain's anecdotes of his experiences drinking ether, just as Lorrain might have taken some inspiration from the "Contes d'Au-Delà."

inert, my mouth closed, my eyes harsh. During the fatal second, when she paused on the threshold of that door, and half-turned, still uncertain, the exact notion of a tomorrow empty of her, of the baseness of my conduct, frightened me. I let her go....

"That was ten months ago; was it not rather yesterday that I sought her svelte form by my side, that I thought I heard the accustomed rustle of her skirt, the faint patter of her footsteps?

"I'll never see her again, except in the chimerical countries of dreams....

"Dead!"

Desirous of escaping the emprise of sterile regret, Pierre decided on the ether.

Soon, he was smiling at prodigious, immeasurable marvels, looming up in the undulating mist of the Imaginary. A whirlwind passed by, swaying its great, dull vapor above the immense gulfs of Infinity, which extend all the way to mauve horizons, divined so distantly that a deliriant vertigo and a superstitious fear emanate from the enormous Space, mingled with attraction. The ground is strewn with the fleecy feathers of birds; it is agitated by slow convulsions, covered with pustules that swell to bursting point and then shrink to tiny bubbles; they vanish. Masses move, creep and change position with sinuous curvaceous deformations; a fiery incandescence floats over the chaos, which becomes more precise.

"You see: up there will scintillate crystal lamps, sparkling chandeliers, from which a sparkling cascade of green and red pendants falls. Painted bayaderes, like frail idols whose thin limbs will be dressed in muslin, run in mosaic frescoes around the rutilant vault. On the square, robust, powerful pillars constellated with bronzed nails, others stand up, columns of cinnabar, on which the sacred image of the Good Goddess is displayed!

"You see, my love, how the turbulent swarm of supple ballerinas dances, provocative wasps in corselets nielloed with light damascenes of shadow—so light! The tambourines groan and the flutes proffer harmonious modulations. At that spectacle, my limbs let go of terrestrial attachments, and I experience an inexpressible joy in no longer perceiving the greasepaint of life, of floating above forgotten human ugliness.

"So stay with me, my love....

"Oh, I once *sensed* that you came in silently, that I interrogated you...you didn't reply. You were cold, for the friction of your fluid vestment touched me...you aren't sitting by the fire....

"Stay close to me; tell me that you've forgotten the fatal moment when I was so nasty....

"If you knew, my love, how I have suffered, how I have wept, how I have cursed my absurd and baleful anger...now, I shall be so humble, so submissive, so tender, that you will love me; we were so happy once! Forgive me, please, forgive me! Beauty! You're still beautiful! Your long hair—how long your hair is!—still shines with an uncertain hint of amethyst or sapphire, which delights me when I see it shining there. And your eyes, your dark eyes—in truth, are they not even darker?—bring to my soul the repose that was once found there. You still have that virginal, alluring hue that your suntanned flesh possessed....

"But where shall I seek that flesh? It's getting dark; yes, it's getting very dark; and I can only perceive, in the darkness, vague pale floating islets....

"Why don't you speak to me? I adore your voice, I adore hearing its fresh and melodious timbre. You remain mute...and the veil enveloping you...? Are you going to take it off, to appear to me radiant and dazzling, dressed as for a fête? And what fête could be more joyful than that! For you're coming back to me, aren't you? You've forgotten you've forgiven? Say something to me; give me a kiss....

"Ah, here's the light, and that ray of moonlight, filtering discreetly, is worth more to me than the radiance of all the suns, since it permits me to see you better....

"You're laughing, I think, you're laughing, and your little pearly teeth are reflecting the light that illuminates them...Heavens! That's horrible! Am I dreaming? No, no, *she's* doing me harm...those fingernails, those pointed fingernails, those dead woman's fingernails, digging into my neck...and that fleshless, bony head, gazing at me with its empty orbits....

"Ah!"

From a motif of weaponry, he snatches an open dagger and strikes at the phantom, desperately.

At the same time, he feels a sharp commotion in his

breast; his shirt becomes sticky with a warm liquid.

Pierre staggers, bewildered, falls in a faint; and, having recovered an uneasy consciousness of the real, dies without understanding that he has killed himself, the victim of a deceptive hallucination, in the course of which, attributing his sensations to a foreign personality, he believed in the actual presence of the abandoned lover, in her macabre transformation, unaware that, in striking out at her, he has only afflicted himself.

The cat moans softly, sniffing the cadaver, while, near the exotic wall-hanging on which a flock of pink flamingoes is traversing capricious clouds, the little Japanese skeleton continues its slow gyration, hanging from the candelabra by a slender thread, which Pierre can no longer see.

THE DEAD MAN'S DREAM

The orders, which were very strict, were followed to the letter, and in spite of their attempts, journalists, students and curiosity-seekers were unable to gain entry to the autopsy room.

In the four corners, four stone tables are set up, extending their mocking gray mass, corroded by brown ulcers, like antique altars. They are exceedingly old, and the soft friction of the cadavers that have lain upon them have varnished them with a patina, as shiny as that distinguishable in the depths of crypts, on funereal paving-stones on which too many people have knelt down. The middle of the room, the chalk-whitened walls of which only reflect the shady light traversing the narrow, barred windows overlooking a garden, which is ornamented in spring by clumps of periwinkles and hollyhocks, is cheered up by the splashing of a fountain whose droplets form a miniature cascade in a shiny metal bowl.

Only the theater assistant was with me, actively occupied, while smoking a short-stemmed pipe, in making a collections of various calculi, which he had carefully sorted out in a tinplate box. Collecting those little stones was his hobby, which he picked up at hazard from abdomens, in the environment of coiling greasy intestines, as one picks up shiny pebbles or nacreous seashells among wet brown tangles of seaweed. Silently, he arranged them, expelling puffs of blue smoke at regular intervals, the acrid odor of which corrected the indefinable and insipid odor floating in the semi-darkness.

After having consulted my watch, whose hands disappointed me by virtue of their slow movement, I allowed a sharp exclamation to escape, expressive of my impatient annoyance. Then he deigned to quit his macabre task momentarily to say to me, after having inspected the sky covered with a diaphanous mantle of morning mist: "He can't be much longer, Monsieur. They must be making casts, and they'll bring him along shortly."

Then, shaking the ashes out of his mouth-burner, he set to work again, methodically.

The overly long wait was aggravating me, truly, and the contemplation of the tables, and the vulgar fountain, with which I was equally familiar, only offered me a mediocre distraction.

The Imaginary then came to my aid, transfiguring the dismal space and real basement; was I not in some temple consecrated to a grim divinity, which demanded a quotidian tribute of human victims, and was not the hour about to sound for the sacrifice that I, as the high priest, would carry out?

And, in fact, Science, which I was honored to serve

in a humble capacity, could easily be represented as that august, mysterious and powerful Idol, since she commands thousands of intellectuals—and not fictitious ones, but people living amid suffering and dolorous labor, shedding blood and tears every day for her, a demanding deity who only delivers her secrets to initiates! How many individuals have prostrated themselves fruitlessly before the Goddess as mute as the sphinx, and died as fervent martyrs for having known her? And as the generations, all ephemeral, have passed away, drunk by the soft sand of Oblivion, she has raised herself up on the fecund alluvia brought by those human waves before they disappeared.

A slight shadow of melancholy was beginning to invade me. I therefore experienced a joyful relief when I heard heavy footsteps approaching and blows shaking the door. I opened it precipitately.

They threw *him* carelessly on to one of the antique blocks, where he rendered a dull thud as he fell, comparable to that produced by a forceful blow with a linen-beater on damp cloth.

He seemed to be very short. The porters stepped back.

"What about the head?" I asked, not seeing it.

"It must be there, Monsieur," replied one of them, untying the bloody sheet.

In fact, it had been placed under his arm.

"Like Saint Denis after the decapitation," said the smiling theater assistant, who was sometimes inclined to be facetious. Becoming serious again, he rolled up his sleeves.

The corpse of the guillotined man had not yet been overtaken by rigor mortis. Warm, supple and robust, the muscles causing bulges in the skin—scarcely splashed in places by a red spume that emphasized its vivid flesh-tint—he lay in a calm and confident attitude, with a beautiful purity of lines; one might have thought him an exhausted wrestler, if the atrocious impression caused by the absence of a face and the scarlet furrow sectioning the neck had not recalled the hideous evidence.

Banal, saddening considerations concerned with the fragility of our existence assailed me in spite of my frequent anterior relations with death. It is true that the majority of the corpses on which I had operated had succumbed after the weakening effects of a slow disease or had been overtaken by accidents that had mutilated them. Others, those of old men, shriveled, thin, paltry, debilitated or deformed—all of them, in sum—presented themselves marbled with the red, green and purple patches of putrefaction, already no longer bearing much resemblance to human form, while *he* was only an hour old...and an infinitesimal fraction of a minute had sufficed to annihilate his vigorous health, his athletic strength and snuff out his life like a candle-flame.

Now, with the ribs broken in a triangle and chest sliced open, where I rummaged between the faded pink lungs to reach the heart, the invaded carcass only made me think about the skinning of some strange animal in a butchery.

While my assistant slowly extracted the marrow—a difficult operation at which he excelled, bringing it out of the vertebrae delicately, as one extracts the succulent flesh from a lobster's claw, I picked up the head of the executed man.

Completely exsanguinated, it was horribly pale, the violet lips thick and sensual and the eyes open, fixed, the blue-green irises tarnished by a thin mist what opalized their transparency. A silky brown tint circled them. I held it in both hands in order to examine it: the enormous frontal sinuses, the nose with a thin deviation in the middle and the protrusive inferior jaw gave the face a bestial appearance completed by jutting cheekbones; all those characteristics formed, by their combination, an accomplished criminal type.

I took a knife that the assistant handed to me and was getting ready to cut through the hairy scalp, in such a fashion as to lay the skull bare before sawing through the bone to reach the brain, when a bizarre noise, composed of articulate, albeit very faint sounds, a buzz of confused words, stopped me.

Surprised, I looked around; the only animate being accompanying me had his mouth closed, and in any case, the timbre of the voice was unknown to me. It seemed impersonal, extra-human, emanating from the very things that it evoked; it was soft and, I should say, perfumed with terror: that expression almost renders the sentiment I had at the time, for it appeared to me that the voice was caressing me with a sepulchral odor, a mixture of incense and putrescence, and a breath of fear.

I do not frighten easily and have never had hallucinations; at that moment, however, I began to doubt myself and my mental lucidity. I felt a vague dread that made my pulse beat faster and squeezed my throat painfully. Certainly, I confess, I was afraid—a crazy fear, giving rise to a desire to flee—and I almost dropped the murderer's head on the floor in that moment of abrupt terror.

Nevertheless, I mastered that sudden panic and, my mouth dry and my temples burning, feeling my heart hammering tumultuously in my breast, I listened to the voice.

At first, I could not make out anything precise. The syllables flowed, stifled and guttural, without the clear pronunciation that would have permitted meaning to be attached to them. They succeeded one another rapidly, reminiscent of the susurrus of the fast-flowing springs that one sometimes encounters in forests, hidden beneath moss and leaves. At the same time, I thought ironically that it was impossible, utterly impossible, for a head, on the one hand separated from the larynx, and on the other hand deprived of the blood indispensable to its functioning, to express ideas that it ought no longer to have; and I mocked myself for my credulous attention in trying to grasp some scrap of a sentence more clearly.

However...you will certainly have found yourself, sometimes, in the course of a heavy nightmare, suddenly transfixed, as it were, by an abrupt, horrible paralysis preventing any action, which robs you, in the presence of an urgent, immediate danger, of any means of self-defense. It gives rise to an immense breathless anguish, and then a plunge into darkness and an awakening.

For me, the scene happened exactly like that.

That which I was holding between my fingers disappeared, or, rather, dissolved in my consciousness along with my own personality. I had the impression—imprecise, to be sure—that I was penetrating into that strange, desert soul, annexing the perceptions, ideas and images abandoned by the other, for whom I substituted myself by means of a sort of taking possession of his former habitat.

Was I *him* or *me*? Perhaps both at the same time, and not doubled; at any rate, I did not ask myself the question. That ambiguous way of being, that equivocal state of mind will doubtless appear to some to be illusory, deceptive and implausible; let it suffice for me to recall that all I am doing now is transcribing, as faithfully as possible, the impressions I had then, without analysis or criticism.

Soon, I sensed an obscure, latent danger threatening, from which I could not run away. My pupils dilated in vain, trying to pierce the darkness, to divine the monstrous peril crouching, lying in wait, protected by the lugubrious opacity that surrounded me, and my lungs inflated extraordinarily in the attempt to relieve the burden of anxiety oppressing them.

A time of transition, empty, for my memory can find nothing therein.

There was, afterwards, the inevitable imminence of the fatal term. I had the intuition that no benevolent, tutelary, charitable force could withdraw me from it.

A square extends, cold and sinister, bordered by leafless trees whose branches establish a network of perforated lace, an extremely fine guipure, beneath the sparkling train of the firmament, dressed with bloody roses and jonquils, brushed by the luminous caress of the breaking dawn. Coral clouds drift over a pearl-gray sky toward golden archipelagos; in the distance, the far distance, tall houses, washed with grayness, with mauve slate roofs, licked by the pale carmine of the rays of the rising star.

On the far side of the empty space, an agitated crowd, noisy and censorious, presses, groaning, behind the lined-up horsemen, sabers held high, speckled with glints; a crowd that I cannot see, but of whose presence the rumor rising from that barrier of guards is sufficient indication.

Why are these human forms dragging me? I don't want to. No, but…I can't succeed in getting rid of the tight cords that are binding me.

Ha! My gaze collides with a machine that I recognize: two shafts framing a shiny triangle. At the same time I sway, precipitated forwards, and I feel the impediment of a rigid and icy collar around my neck.

The blade is taking a long time—or are these seconds counting double? I'd like to collect myself, to obtain one last lucid, solemn thought before the final moment...everything is floating, indecisive, fluid in my head, which is about to fall....

However, naïve and candid images now pass by— with an inconceivable rapidity that does not exclude a complete precision of detail—of my actions as a little child, trivial episodes dating from my infancy, their insignificance magnified and retained, young faces and the primitive landscapes forming them.

That revivification of exceedingly ancient memories radiates like a spray of bursting skyrockets, a constellation rapidly eclipsed.

An indefinable sensation of emptiness follows a violent impact on the nape of the neck; I can clearly perceive the absence of my body, and the strangeness of that observation frightens me.

The black splashed with red and the red striped with black beneath my eyelids, palpitating with an irrepressible flutter...a remembrance of the most recent impression, the bisection of the cutter slicing through the marrow, drilling me with a shrill dolor...all that survives of the final collapse.

Here there is a period of absolute, complete unconsciousness, following which, progressively, I descend once again into myself; a soft warmth, an infinite well-being, reanimates me, penetrates me, and I rediscover myself in my laboratory, pouring orange liquid over a brain placed in a crystallizer.

Surprised and frightened, I look around attentively; everything is in its place and there is no possible confusion. That microscope is mine; I made use of those bottles yesterday. How, then, did that incursion into a strange soul, that transfusion in which I must have run through once again the emotional phases preceding his death, not interrupt all my actions?

What has happened?

I have interrogated my assistant. He did not notice anything at all abnormal about me. I persist; he maintains his reply. He has seen me continuing the necropsy, taking the anatomical specimens and return to the building where I now am, in order to place them in the customary solution to harden.

It's true, then! A part of my being applied itself to its occupations, while another relived a terrifying agony.

Well, yes! That funereal phantasmagoria, coexistent with multiple tasks, although not necessitating an intelligent collaboration, is possible; and, after due reflection, I ought not to be so surprised, being aware of cases of that sort, having observed them, and knowing their mechanism.

Even so, an anxious astonishment pursues me; I resemble a man whose knows the geography of a country perfectly, from having read exact topographical descriptions of it, and who finds himself transported to the place itself; I believe that, in spite of his anterior notions, he would nevertheless feel out of place.

And I catch myself doubting that singular dream, searching for fearful and superstitious interpretations.

I shall take a bromide this evening.

THE LAMP

16 October 18**

"My lamp only went out very slowly.

"Between the moment when I commenced to perceive that its light was diminishing in intensity and the one when I was plunged into darkness, there were insensible, inappreciable degradations: a lapse of time went by, which I am unable to calculate exactly. Sometimes, my memories, which remain very vague on this point, represent it to me as of a considerable duration, at other times it appears to me as having been very short.

"Whatever the interval might have been, precisely, in which the extravagant scene unfolded—of which I can no longer think without terror—I cannot form an exact notion of it. No, in truth, I cannot.

"Now, by the warm and dying light of the flame— it vacillated with tremors of agony—I fixed my gaze, certainly at random but very attentively, on the center of the cloth covering my table. The cloth was green; a rather dark green; it was patterned by yellow arabesques.

"At the same time, I repeated to myself in a

whisper—by what whom was I moved, I wonder?—the syllables of my name: 'Lou…is Bru…nel…. Lou…is Bru…nel….'

"Suddenly, it appeared to me that a part of my being, made up of my intimate personality, of that which seemed to me to constitute, after a fashion, the very essence of my self, entirely spiritual—let's call it my soul—had become detached from my body, which remained seated, head bowed, eyes staring, lips still murmuring 'Lou…is Bru…nel….'

"Floating above it, I gazed at myself thus, from slightly higher up and to the right.

"I had a complete consciousness of that abandonment, but even so, it could hardly help but surprise me. Without succeeding, I sought to take better account of that singular state. Ideas reached me weakly, confused, like the rambling dreams of an invalid. I found myself changed, *other* than before; objects, even familiar ones, took on unusual appearances for my new self, and I looked back incessantly, with an increasing, indescribable anxiety, at my material form, which maintained its fixity of attitude in its immobility.

"Oh, what a vast pride I experienced in considering it thus, in being liberated from that envelope. Empty of all spirit, did it not conserve nothing of me but the name? And I was scornful of it, glad to feel myself transported in an atmosphere of dream, disengaged from any *heavy* reality.

It was definitely that sensation of lightness, of distance from the normal world—until then, the only one I had known—that struck me most forcibly. I began to think then that the change of milieu made me into a new being, that the soul, irreducible so far as space was concerned, must also be irreducible in respect of time. Immediately, although very imprecise at first, something analogous to a memory of a similar anterior existence passed rapidly by, and then a conviction formed with regard to it. Was it not plausible to suppose myself a prisoner of successive incarnations, only one of which still responded to the appeal of consciousness?

"For although I tried in vain to remember the details of my past lives, I only obtained an affirmation of their reality; a forceful affirmation, without my knowing more surely on what it was based.

"Where and when had I lived previously? Those questions remained unanswered; but that relative ignorance did not shake my general conviction and, drawing that certainty nearer, I recognized in the present fact a confirmation—tangible, so to speak—of moral beliefs and religious ideas that had been inculcated in me in infancy, in the immortality of the soul.

"Very happy to have recovered a long lost faith, I was invaded by an inexpressible contentment, an immense joy. Death, hideous Death, could therefore do nothing to us; was it not the separation that I was observing, bringing nothing except the very pleasant and not justifying the stupid fear of the majority of people? Yes, I rediscovered the liberation of which certain philosophers and a few poets have spoken. Why be frightened of deceptive appearances, by the repugnant decomposition of a body, no longer having, simply by virtue of the fact that it is corruptible, anything in common with the soul, our unique self, our intimate essence, our very individuality?

"Thus, the human form that I had inhabited, by means of which I had lived, suffered and loved, was bound for annihilation, to be dissolved back into the great crucible, from which it would scatter its volatile atoms, henceforth devoid of cohesion. Soon, nothing would remain of it, not even a memory, since my memory was localized within it, as proven by its silence on the matter of an anterior existence.

"And I would doubtless bring to life and consciousness another aggregate of molecules: which? and how? and why...?

"Momentarily, I had lifted the veil of the mysterious and future Isis; I thought I could already perceive her resplendent divinity, finally knowing the solution to those problems in which the unknown hides from our ever-insufficient interpretations—and then weight fell back, the indecipherable web, leaving me by virtue of that fall to wander once again in shadows denser than obscurity, and rapidly returning doubt. Confronted by that inability to know any more than the present, I was gripped by a horrific anguish.

"What god or what fatality, then, pushes beings into blindness, without permitting them to see and to hope? Captives of eternal error, ignorant of the supreme goal of their efforts and whether their efforts even have a goal, how do they know that, for myriads of centuries, generations have not been agitating in vain in an impenetrable Nothing surrounding them on all sides?

"Oh, the poignant bite of impotence, which cruelly tore me away from the contemplation of the rigid silhouette, blurred by the decreasing and feeble light of the already-smoky wick.

"There was a *being* there, having thought and desired, whose eyes had wept sterile tears, whose lips had sketched futile smiles!—a human, a grain of the animate dust that time strews incessantly through space; a deplorable and utterly ignorant mass of contradictions, whose unconsciousness and inexpressible fatuity was proud of knowing and measuring all its infinitesimal limits! When that form had dissolved, everything would have been said about the creature that occupied it.

"But then, what would I become, myself? Was the dissociation that I had observed momentarily, of the two elements that I had considered to one person, definitive? In that case, why linger over the spectacle of my physical envelope, surely dead?

"It was at the exact moment when I posed that question that the unexpected phenomenon occurred that has haunted me obsessively ever since.

"For scarcely a second, the exceedingly dark room was violently illuminated.

"In front of me, on the wall, in the full glare of the light, was one of those common-or-garden calendars whose leaves are designed to be torn off, which had nothing unusual about it. It bore the date: *Wednesday 15 October* in large black letters.

"I then saw, quite distinctly, a hand tear away several leaves, until *23 November* appeared.

"At that moment, the half-hour chimed on my clock....

"The lamp went out and I cannot remember any more."

17 October
"This morning, I searched carefully, everywhere for the vanished pages; I could not find them...."

"Such is the narrative, written by Louis Brunel, that I found in the course of the investigation that I was obliged to conduct on the subject of his violent death. By a strange coincidence, on the twenty-third of November, a fire took hold in his bedroom, caused, without a doubt, by the fall of a lamp placed next to the bed.

"The cadaver was partly charred, but the head, somewhat spared by the flames, did not display the grimacing expression that it is usual to encounter in such cases. On the contrary, it retained a calm, slightly smiling, expression, as if the pain had not even been felt. The right hand, which was intact, was holding in its clenched fingers the pages of a calendar from the fifteenth of October to the very day of the accident.

"The clock had stopped on the half-hour."

Distractedly leafing through the dead man's manuscript, Dr. Nervis fell silent, while he interrogated

Maurice de Hautval with his gaze.

"To tell the truth," the young man replied, "it seems to me that we are straying, thanks to that unfortunate fellow, into a labyrinth of errors and half-truths. There is a darkness therein that the vacillating flame of Reason is insufficient to dissipate, a darkness that extends before us and closes in behind us, without any thread provided by a benevolent Ariadne. Are we not groping our way forward, bent double, because the impenetrable vault of Reality is too low to permit is to walk upright? We bump into it when we extend our arms. Yes, Louis Brunel is right; your science is vain, remaining perpetually incomplete and false, mute to prayer, and cannot give us either hope or confidence!"

"I have no hesitation, my dear Maurice, in recognizing with you that often, behind clearly visible phenomena, the great figure of the Unknown, the Mysterious, looms up, still inexplicable, divined rather than sensed. But if Hypothesis moves quickly along its path, if the Imaginary is rapidly forced to find a solution, satisfactory in appearance and sufficient, in fact, for many simple minds or those too hasty to reach a conclusion, it is not the same for the science that you seem to disdain. It begins by ensuring unshakable foundations before constructing its work, on which thousands of laborers are working incessantly.

"By the combination of those simultaneous efforts—a slow combination, to be sure, but conscientious and strong, because it only advances at a sure tread and not very far on solid and prepared terrain—it gradually raises up the edifice of knowledge, increasing its growth without fear that it might crumble, without the pretention of finishing at a single stroke and right away.

"Besides which, in the case that concerns us, everything can, it seems to me, be brought within the scope of known laws; given that, there is nothing supernatural about it. Still, it's necessary to know the laws in question!

"I'm not talking to you, Maurice, in particular, but about how, by authorizing vague notions, and not finding in them, for good reason, the solution of any complex problem, they can be declared irreducible to scientific data, rejected by virtue of that fact into the realm—vast enough without that—of the inexplicable!

"Now, Louis Brunel presented, so far as I was able to judge when I treated him, symptoms emerging from a neurosis that as once thought to be the exclusive privilege of women, the frequency of which in men, perhaps even greater, has been demonstrated by recent research: hysteria. Among other signs of that affliction, he offered the complete insensitivity of an entire side, in his case the right, that is ordinarily found in that sort of malady; and on the other hand, crises the nature of which there is no doubt.

"What happened on the fifteenth of October?

"Louis Brunel falls, as a result of circumstances that he has indicated himself, into one of these fits, which, according to the description that he has left us, contains all the characteristics of *hysterical vigil-*

ambulism.[4] You know, moreover, that that state of the doubling of the personality, which possesses analogies extending almost as far as equivalence with hypnotic sleep, is tantamount to an attack of hysteria.

"It is during that second state that, with his anesthetized limb, the movements of which he cannot, in consequence, perceive, he tears the leaves from the calendar. He then sees a hand carrying out that action, and cannot conceive of the hand as his own, since he received no sensation of it. Thus, it seems to him to be action of another.

"The next day, having come round, he is extremely impressed by the lacuna presented by the calendar, and, by virtue of that excitement, the scene he has played out the previous day returns vaguely to his consciousness. Note in that respect the abundance with which he extends himself upon the details preceding it, and the relative brevity of the subject of the principal part of the story.

"For more than a month the date 23 November remains before his eyes; what is astonishing in the fact of the production, by virtue of that obsession, in a subject thus predisposed, of a veritable autosuggestion, from which results, on the day indicated, the recurrence of a doubtless-analogous fit?

"In the course of the new crisis, the events that have taken place during the previous one return as precise memories—which is the rule. That explains the facility with which he rediscovers the detached pages, which

---

4. Vigilambulism is a state similar to somnambulism, but which occurs while its victim is awake rather than asleep

he was incapable of doing in a waking state.

"The attack terminates, as usual, in a few convulsive gestures, to which we should probably attribute the final accident, the fall of the lamp, provoking the fire in which he dies. The serenity of the expression relates, naturally, to the semi-anesthesia of the right side. As for the precise time, the reason is simpler still: the heat developed at the moment of the catastrophe, which stopped the clock!"

IN VAIN

It was in the evening that the encounter, now unforgettable, took place. of which I retain precisely, almost by way of an obsession, the quotidian vision of the landscape that witnessed the event: the place where the event occurred that I would now assume to have been a dream, or rather a nightmare, if the daily vision of a place that remains exactly similar, and toward which a stupid force urges me every day to return, did not keep reminding me that it was real.

The region is almost unknown, and primitive; perhaps that is why I like it—but the sea also exercises the seductions of a lover upon me. Away from her, I experience a painful sensation of emptiness; I miss its sounds, ample and attractive, majestic and tender, the lullaby that its waves sing to sandy beaches, at the angles of which the pale brown profiles of cliffs loom up. For it isn't the calm tideless waves that I desire, the blue lake that bathes the shores of sunny regions and golden archipelagos; I want the moving immensity, advancing with glaucous menaces, perfidious undulations, enlacing the reefs in their powerful grip, to flee thereafter, slowly, abandoning a carpet of brown algae to lacy foam, withdrawing to open water, not without abrupt returns and long kisses.

How many hours were spent thus in horizontal reveries on the rough ridges of rocks, caressed by the breeze, impregnated with humid dust, which leaves its saline trace on the lips, bitter and yet sweet! The ambience embalmed with the perfume of gorse and heather, and no importunate intruder to trouble my pleasant solitude. Better than the cicadas, better than the birds of the fields, the song of forgotten and noisy seashells accompanied delightfully vague dreams, hatching out in the random breezes, while the undulating waves played with them, speckled with silvery gleams.

That day, the equinoctial low tide of the Ocean had uncovered an unusual span, and I was wandering through the pale green and pink mosses, the prodigiously fine lacework, paneling the flints. Beneath their thin filigree, there were translucent and fulgurant colorations, which oscillated between the somber lacquer-work: carmines edged with snowy fire, bright vermilion reds and incandescent violets, soft lilacs heightened by coral hems, speckled here and there with scarlet patches. Marine lianas, wracks interlaced their serpentine networks, composing a darker carpet of Havana velvet, in which ran multiple glints of amber and bright ocher, contrasting with the bitumen of the clearly excised shadows. Sometimes, on the edge of a hiatus, on a ridge, a crab raised up its arachnid structure, ceasing to run obliquely to rear up, motionless and anxious, in the curiously detailed posture of a

Japanese bronze. Through the water of little limpid pools, sparkling like polished metal mirrors, diaphanous transparent shrimp were swimming gracefully, in abrupt fits and starts, with lovely curving movements of their antennae; sea anemones were vibrating all their thin and numerous animal-flower filaments, and slender fish, like rapid black streaks, were darting back and forth, rippling the flat surfaces of the pools.

One might have thought it the supernatural décor of an ideal fairyland, transporting you with its supreme, unreal esthetic, its beauty, far from the hideous, narrow and dull banality of paltry human conceptions, which it crushed with all its august, magnificent grandeur, and its placid, enormous, unconscious strength. Like monstrous animals with stony spines and limbs of granite, the rocks were evocative, resounding with the eternal battle fought against the waves, shaken by the muffled blows of the formidable battering-ram, undermining them relentlessly, and the echoes multiplying a hundredfold the noise of crumbling shingle and dragged pebbles, streaming in cascades.

In spite of the rumor of the waves, however, I perceived a plaintive human voice, which reached me, and through a breach separating the stratifications that loomed up far enough to mask the sky, I perceived the desolate individual in question.

A few strides permitted me to get close enough to see and hear.

"A little while ago," he murmured, "I met a little child on the beach who was crying very loudly. Why?

I don't know…little children cry like that for trivial reasons. Certainly, I envied, madly, the lot of that little boy with the curly hair, and his tears, because he could shed tears, as many as he liked, while I would dearly love to weep, but no longer can—and yet it's necessary that I weep, for I feel pity now, in stifling the tears; my heart is heavy, so heavy with dolorous compassion, that it almost fill my entire breast, and oppression squeezes my throat. It seems to me that that anguish might disappear if I were able to weep. Ha ha! Isn't it singular: I'm becoming compassionate and lamenting. Me! Me…*me!*"

It was in a fearful tone that the man had articulated the final syllable. He was sitting on a rock, gripping his forehead with both hands, thus hiding his eyes, and the glory of the sunset surrounded him with an atmosphere of bronze, flamboyant beneath a violet dome, slashed by bloody and raw wounds opened in the flanks of the heavens, without his seeming to perceive that splendor. The sea was shining with triumphant, dazzling colors, as if decked in a luminous adornment of red and gold pouring out from the distant dusk, discovering the mass of granitic heaps, which, extending along one side of the sand, bathed on the other by the waves, gave the appearance of some enormous beast, fissured by numerous cuttings, carved with breaches and gashes, but victorious even so, constraining the haughty, resplendent and growling waves to recoil after licking its feet.

Suddenly, the occidental gleams diminished in

intensity, and the reign commenced of soft shades, nuanced in dreamy hues, nacreous sparkles and iridescent clouds. Mists appeared out at sea, which glided softly over the quivering, pearly water, and shadows descended from the firmament, striped with frail clouds like muslin scarves, which blurred the harsh contours and fissures of the rocks. Not far away from us, a seagull screeched; at that noise, the man's hands uncovered his face; his yellow irises shot a long glance in that direction.

Now, I was there, but he did not see me.

He did not see me; he certainly had not seen me when his eyes seemed to look around in that fashion, and yet, on remembering the impression I had then, and remembering the sound of his voice, and the moment when he began speaking again, I still feel frightened, for what that man proffered engendered fear. The Word emerged from his lips, and I knew that I ought not to be listening like that, but a crazy desire to know the entire horrible past of that stranger rose within me, and a paralyzing, absurd terror prevented me from accomplishing any movement, from going away, even though I knew that I was doing something bad.

In addition, everything he said was terrifying, and the wild frame in which we found ourselves added even further to my frisson of horror.

He continued:

"Well, yes, me, me! The respected and venerable old man, a man of integrity; and why be astonished that a feeble old man should complain and want to weep?

He's certainly not the same person as the vigorous, young, robust individual who....

"I don't know why I'm hesitating; I'm alone here—and who, in any case, would take any notice of the divagations of a white-bearded madman? No, I'm no longer the man who...has killed!

"Oh, the funereal vision that unfolds, like a tapestry, the characters of which, embroidered in antique silks, belonging to the past, have half-faded away into the worn weave, only conserving the incomplete gestures and pale attitudes appropriate to discolored phantoms! And what reproaches, what grim reproaches there are in that mute evocation of distant, almost forgotten deaths; how eloquently the gaping mouths speak, the convulsed limbs, the eyes swiveling in their orbits! And I once delighted in the contemplation of those open breasts; I only left the profaned cadavers with the regret of not having extracted other joys therefrom....

"Today, I would like to weep, perhaps for the irreparable deaths, perhaps for the brute I was!

"How did all that happen? One day, an absolute change occurred, deep inside my self, in the manner of those transformations of scene that are operated in the theater, behind the lowered curtain. The canvas has been raised in me, and I can no longer take account of that which exists; and I do not understand that which is.

"By what magic, then, has this new being been substituted for the other, whom I sense living in the stead of the old, and who is critical of him? Everything in my soul is tumultuous, contradictory and obscure, and a storm-wind has whipped up the mud of ancient memories there, which were reposing under the deceitful, fictive dead water of forgetfulness. To be unable to detach from one's memory, the impartial spectator, those vestiges of another self! And with what clarity I see myself again!

"For a long time I had been subject to that homicidal temptation and had struggled against the invincible attraction of murder, when the sun rose one morning and it became impossible for me to struggle. From then on, I sought out victims in order to sacrifice them to that passion, which seemed to have so many attractions. To kill! That seemed to me so sweet…and in reality I know—the confession burns my lips today— yes, I knew all its intoxication, all its enchantment, all its voluptuousness.…

"The first was a little boy, very blond, with pretty and cheerful dark eyes.

"Woe!

"I promised him a few marbles, and succeeded thus in drawing him far away from the town. We walked along remote paths—at any rate, I didn't meet anyone— and he chattered all the way, bringing me flowers he had picked. His pleasure made me laugh, for as soon as we arrived in the wood, as we were alone, I grabbed him by the throat…oh that skin, so soft and so warm, palpitating under the grip!

"He was already weary, and scarcely put up a fight. Now, I remember clearly, I squeezed slowly, excited to the marrow of my bones, gazing at that dainty figure, convulsed by fear, expressing supreme terror. When I let him go, he was no longer moving.

"That wasn't yet sufficient. I wanted to see blood, to see the viscous flood seething out of the arteries, and I mutilated that poor body with such joy that, when I got home, I couldn't stop myself from writing down, immediately, the thought that haunted me: *to kill a child is good, and warm!*

"Damnation! To think that that can never be effaced, never disappear...never again, and even if others remain ignorant forever, I shall know. Is it possible that my present self is that of old? No, not a single material atom of him survives, and I can raise my head: the other is dead and I haven't retained anything of him, since he moves me to pity, since, whenever I remember the man who was me, an immense commiseration overwhelms me, to the point of anguish...."

And I thought: insensate, a man who desires to weep for himself and proclaims that he has not inherited any legacy from his primitive personalities, when all his thoughts return to the past, and he cannot forget. In truth, he'd like to annihilate that memory within him, but that memory is his life, and was his happiness! It was his happiness; he was happy then—atrociously happy. He is no longer.

Is that remorse?

No, I thought, remorse can only exist under the title of fiction; one does not regret joyous intoxication; one only regrets not having enjoyed more of it, or, when it is a matter of that which crime procures, having enjoyed it. The sentiment torturing him is the consciousness of change, that of not remaining identical to himself.

On reflection, I thought, his dolor could be applied with as much reason to his present self as to that of yesterday, since, once one was separated from the other, he would be calm, not tormented; it was precisely that coexistence of the two enemy individualities that was harassing him with torments, to which he would doubtless have preferred the cruelest of physical tortures.

The man moaned, moaned in the plaintive tone of a desolate woman.

With a noise comparable to the gallop of a hundred furious horses carried away by a mad stampede, whose hooves were treading on sonorous paving-stones, the waves were returning. Soon, the spray of the surf would begin to reach me, similarly constraining the unknown man to retreat.

Against the milky horizons where the ocean and sky were confused in a single pale mist, the man profiled the arc of his tall, curved silhouette. He walked, haloed with silver by the rays of the moon, which played in the curls of his hair; tall, serene and dignified, he walked like a patriarch of the ancient times of innocence, and behind his steps, the foam-striped eddies rushed from all directions, launching themselves seething on this heels, as if his presence had thus far held back that invasion. Meanwhile, beneath soft blue satin vellum heightened by the rich braid of constellations surrounding the blond star, he climbed the broad rough-hewn foundations of fantastic architectures of darkness preceding the cliff.

And, taking on the appearance of a supernatural accusation, emerging from objects themselves, the voice resounded again, in conformity with the lugubrious scene that the sinister actor was playing.

"What's the point of berating oneself or moaning? Whatever I do, no matter how pure and full of good works my final years might be, it will always be impossible for me to erase that page of the book of my life. And it's an illusory task that I'm undertaking in wanting to erase it.

"Anyway, no base, self-interested, avaricious motive has ever guided my actions, and it was in moments of madness that I must have killed. Others, if they knew how my crimes had been committed, would absolve me, but me, I torture myself pointlessly by trying, like them, to separate the criminal madman from the righteous, honest and sane being that I've never ceased to be outside of those hideous fits. On the contrary, it appears to me that the madman and the sage are only a single individual, that that individual is me, and that all my efforts to judge otherwise are annihilated by memory, remaining vain.

"Certainly, I know that all is vanity, that all activity spread over the earth is a deceptive and ironic mask, which cannot hide the nothingness. I know that all human endeavors are sterile, like those of the elements, like the stupid course of these squalls, like the incessant and aimless movement of the sea; I know that all is vanity, and that that phrase, more than three thousand years old, has lost none of its meaning, and because of that I know that my torture will never end, for I must renounce any attempt at forgetfulness—but there I collide with the constant preoccupation, which incessantly brings me back to dolorous returns upon myself, and I never succeed in obtaining that scission between the abominable past and the present.

"Oh, the little child that was weeping this morning on the beach!

"I want so much to weep!"

A cold north-easterly breeze was blowing from the heath like extra-human laughter; under that powerful breath, a thicket of thorny furze bent over, almost mockingly.

Then everything became calm again, and the unknown man disappeared into the warm poem of peace that the night was singing.

IN ANIMA VILI

The name of Dr. Hirnberg, professor in the Faculty of Medicine at X***, a corresponding member of the Académie de Médecine de Paris and numerous other European scientific societies was not unknown to many. The professor's work on hypnotic suggestion and psychotherapy had, in fact, produced a considerable sensation at one time, which extended beyond purely medical limits, and that notoriety further increased the immense surge of curiosity provoked, shortly after his death, by the clause in his will that a newspaper less discreet than well-informed rendered public.

"I have," he said therein, "deposed on 25 June 18**, in the bureau of the Académie de Médecine de Paris, a sealed envelope containing a note relative to a significant experiment in suggestion; I desire that it be opened during the session of the week following my death."

The delay having expired, in conformity with the wishes of the deceased, the seals enclosing the manuscript were broken before a numerous audience by the secretary of the illustrious assembly, who then read the posthumous communication.

I did not think, *the late professor wrote*, that I ought to publish during my lifetime the observation that I have the honor of submitting to the enlightened judgment of the Académie. That reluctance was not dictated to me, I hasten to say, either by the desire to avoid free discussion—my conduct will, in any case, suffice to exculpate me from that suspicion—nor a desire to escape a grave responsibility—I was resolved from the outset to submit it—but solely by the dread of probably seeing regrettable arguments surge forth regarding the scientific legitimacy of the fact, and especially the fear that the publication in question might lend an undoubtedly false interpretation that would be capable nevertheless of causing a scandal, the dishonor of which, rebounding on the institution, risked tarnishing it reputation.

Have I the right to hope that the appreciation of the facts here reported will be governed by a better impartiality if they remain, as it were, impersonal, their observer having abandoned the land of the living? The respect that surrounds the memory of those who are to more appears to me to be a sure guarantee of that impartiality, for it preserves from a hasty temerity the judgments brought against them.

The experiment that will be described in these notes offers an interest that you will appreciate; it is the first that clarifies precisely, in a new light, and uncontestably fixes the reality of a phenomenon thus far disputed by the majority and only admitted with reservations by others. Furthermore, it required all the force of my desire to establish the objective basis of this exceedingly controversial scientific fact for me to dare to think of undertaking the experiment.

I shall not be telling my scientific colleagues anything new in reminding them of the famous dispute that arose between two major schools shortly after the introduction of hypnotism in the medical domain, even though, for the younger ones among them, the memory is of little more than purely historical interest. What limits ought one attribute to suggestion from the point of view of penal responsibility? Are Charcot, Brouardel and Delboeuf in the right, for whom a somnambulist only ever realizes suggestions agreeable or indifferent to him, or at any rate not in opposition to his education and his character, or Liébault, Beaunis and Liégeois, who contend that in certain subjects the automatism is absolute, that the impulsion to action is irresistible, and, in consequence, that responsibility is nullified?

Drawn by the nature of my works toward this kind of research, I followed all the ups and downs of that debate passionately, checking the assertions of both parties by means of a series of experimental studies of which mention is made in the first volume of my *Essais sur Hypnose*. For me, the question remained in the balance for a long time, and, no more than the authors I have cited, I had not encountered any categorical fact capable for furnishing me with an irrefutable solution, when a serious incident occurred in my private life.

At that time, I had already been married for some years, when a dolorous hazard informed me that my wife had been unable to resist the seduction of adultery. It is cruel for me to confess here the thoughts that assailed me at that moment. However, I owe you an exact report, being only too well aware of the necessity of bringing complete sincerity to the matter, and perhaps the knowledge of the psychology of similar states of mind is equal in value to the experiment that I propose to set before you. Although, I repeat, it costs me dearly to lay bare the secret parts of my soul in this manner, I confess that, while the sentiment immediately experienced was one of profound dolor, mingled with hatred and ideas of vengeance against the wretched accomplice, that affliction did not last long. I was at that time dominated by the passion inspired in me by my research on suggestion, to the point that the thought immediately came into my mind, rather confusedly at first, of attempting an experiment that was not a laboratory exercise. Did not the life of that man belong to me, as much by natural law as by social law, and was there not an unrivaled opportunity to produce, *in anima vili*, the decisive experiment?

Although these sentiments might seem inhuman to you, *a priori*, you will allow me to justify them at least insofar as to avoid any reproach regarding illogicality or cruelty, and even the suspicion of such criticism. You will not expect me, nevertheless, to evoke sentimental arguments before you, any more than to represent myself to you as some kind of agent of stern justice, in the fashion of one of the heroes of Lope de Vega or Corneille, estimating that only a baptism of blood is capable of effacing the outrage done to his honor. On the one hand, I have always maintained, in my life and my writings, that the principle of talion is primitive, unworthy of a civilized era; on the other hand, I have often professed the absurdity of those doctrines—too easily accepted alas—which tend to see a penalty as a compensation: a redemption of crime—irreparable, in essence, by crime—or as a necessary punishment, although the right to punish has no foundation and the punishment itself an inexcusable act of barbarism. Thus, I could not, without a serious dereliction of principles to which I am attached, avoid by those banal considerations a responsibility that I would not dream of denying. Moreover, I am determined to give you a clear explanation of the reasons that dictated the thought in question to me, as mentioned above, and which militated in favor of the action, and its logical, rigorous and legitimate consequence, that I then undertook, and propose to submit to you for your appreciation.

In the matter of adultery, if we examine that lack of laws, making a *tabula rasa* of all false sentimentality, and not granting access to considerations of self-esteem, personal vanity, anger or any egotistic ideas contrary to that of pure justice, we cannot fail to perceive that, envisaged solely under the aspect as a social misdemeanor, it does not cause any grave damage or serious harm to the public, and only supposes a fairly minor degree of criminality on the part of its authors. Thus, to punish that crime by death, as certain outraged husbands do, has always seemed to me to be excessive. How, you have the right ask me, could I thus have put myself in contradiction with my own theories?

Well, the contradiction is only apparent.

I consider, in fact, that it is simultaneously puerile, illusory and dangerous to deviate from the conventions of the society of which one is a part. For example, I would criticize a capitalist who, convinced of the real misery surrounding him and of the baneful influence of his fortune, in spontaneously ridding himself of it, imagines that he is accomplishing an equitable act, when, in reality, his conduct would result in leaving him unjustly disarmed in the bitter struggle for existence. Now, observing my inability to reform, for my part, the inequity to which I was witness, I could, on the other hand, by conforming to social laws, obtain a profit for a nobler end than the one generally served by banal vengeance. It is nonetheless just to recognize that the hope of finally obtaining positive result, after years of work and hesitant trials, and the scientific attraction of such a proof, were not unconnected with my determination, from which, I imagine, emerged the satisfaction that did not take long to succeed my initial prostration.

On 18 April 18**, at six o'clock in the evening, the trial was attempted in my laboratory, to which I had invited L***, one of the subjects, a male hysteric, the detailed observation of whom can be found on page 147 of the third volume of my *Essais sur l'Hypnose*. At that time, the man in question, although no longer directly under my care, was willing to hold himself at my disposition whenever I needed him for my experiments. I chose him for the accomplishment of my plan as much by reason of his perfectly honest antecedents and his mild and timid character, known to me for a long time, as the facility with which he could be subjected to a profound degree of hypnosis. On several occasions—the fact is recorded in his observation—I had noted his realization of a post-hypnotic suggestion, even after a considerable delay. I put him to sleep by my standard method and took him to the second phase of that sleep. In that state, I intimated to him formally, and repeatedly, the order to kill: he would kill; he would want to kill; he could not do otherwise, etc.

I succeeded in making him accept the suggestion, after resistance and negations that lasted no less than thirty-five minutes. I remarked that, in the brief intervals between my reiterations of the order, a struggle seemed to be established within the apparently-doubled personality of the subject, for intermittent exclamations escaped his lips: "Me, kill? …I must!" pronounced in different tones.

When I was certain that an absolute submission was established on his part, I gave him precise details as to the execution. Furthermore, L***, already possessed by the idea, spontaneously asked: "Kill whom?" I indicated explicitly to him the person he was to strike, but at that moment I perceived that, in my preoccupation, I had neglected to prepare the necessary weapon. So, desirous of not prolonging the session unduly, I handed him an autopsy hammer that lay on the table of the laboratory. That negligence presently constitutes a material proof of the reality of the fact.

Naturally, I fixed in the most precise fashion the place where the murder was to be committed, and even indicated to L*** the manner in which to proceed with the attack. It was only after having had each of the episodes of the scene—whose performance I ordered for five hours thereafter—scrupulously rehearsed, so to speak, that I awoke the subject.

He assured me, as usual, that he did not remember anything.

I learned the following day of the success of the experiment: the murder appeared to have been accomplished in the exact conditions that I had determined, and medico-legal expertise demonstrated that the victim had succumbed to the consequences of a fracture of the occipital produced by a blunt instrument of exactly the same form as an autopsy hammer—a fact that struck the medical examiners in the course of their investigation. I did not have to intervene to exonerate L***, who did not come under suspicion, having had no motive. The affair, of which details can easily be found in the newspapers of April 18**, had no judiciary consequences.

Subsequently, L***, when I interrogated him about that night, only reported that he had doubtless had one of the nervous crises to which he was accustomed, during which he had suffered a nose-bleed, as sometimes happened, for he had woken up very tired and his hands bore traces of blood. Put into a somnambulistic state, however, he described the scene of the murder fearfully, and I was able to render account, by virtue of that new evidence, of the absolute value of the post-hypnotic suggestion in question.

This fact therefore constitutes the first scientific observation establishing the effective and complete realization of a crime suggested during hypnosis. It demonstrates that a real murder can be accomplished punctiliously by a subject, then transformed into a veritably impulsive individual, who has unhesitatingly executed a criminal suggestion.

MOUSMÉ
(A DREAM)[5]

I.
The Wait

Light emanated from the sky, a forehead bandaged with pale cloth, still bloodied by the red of the recent sunset, descended upon the sea and enveloped the rocks and sands with a shroud of radiance. Far out in the bay, toward the other shore, the silhouette of whose coast could be divined, lost in the mist, milky smoke was undulating over the slumbering waters, rippled by tremors. When the beams of light reached those clouds, there was a sudden and magnificent transformation; the pallid, dull veils were stirred into pearly sheets, revealing the infinity of silver-splashed horizons, and the waves streamed like a broad torrent

---

5. Author's note: "At the beginning of certain mental afflictions, the subjects sometimes find their sleep obsessed by a dream, always the same, often very eventful, and which can be repeated for months or even years. That repetition permits its most infinitesimal details to be perceived, and, more particularly, preserved from the forgetfulness that usually affects almost all dreams. It has been given to us to discover one of the imaginary episodes of this category—a recurrent dream—written by the patient himself, and it is from his manuscript that the following narrative is directly derived. G.D."

of gold jewelry. Then the moon appeared in its turn, emerging from the screen of clouds, and the scenery emerged from the shadows, finally displayed in its entirety, in its tranquil glory, in the silent and calm peace of that summer evening.

Thérèse clapped her hands ecstatically, and, addressing her companion in reverie, said: "Oh, look! Isn't it cleverly contrived and splendidly successful, that effect!"

"Yes," the young man replied. "This is how I love the night, ornamented and resplendent, in the manner of the princesses of legend, as soft and smiling as them. In her other aspect, as a vile witch in mourning-dress, she frightens me, for I retain from my childhood, rendered timorous by terrors, the memories of the evil tricks she played on me, and I still experience today a justified mistrust, a real fear, with regard to the hours inhabited by nightmares crouching in the darkness."

"But why does darkness seem so redoubtable to you? When I was a child, I too was told tales of werewolves and evil bogey-men, but nothing remains of them but ridiculous memories and a slightly ironic pity for the little girl who was frightened by such scarecrows."

"I don't like to talk about that period of my past, because it remains sensible and dolorous, and I don't like to think about the terrors I experienced then." In a lower voice, as if talking to himself, he went on: "I've been told that I was four years old when, for the first time. I woke up about two hours after I had been put to bed, uttering a loud scream. My mother immediately ran to me, and I still don't know how to explain what had happened to me. After that, every night—every single one, you hear—the same horrible dream that woke me up with a start came back."

"Without pause?"

"It never failed to manifest itself. Every night! So I can't think about that period of my life without it presenting itself to me darkened by that long torture."

"But what was this vision that caused you so much anguish?"

"I found myself crouching at the foot of a wall: a strange, semi-transparent wall; I could perceive, in fact, confusedly, what was happening on the other side. Soon, through that wall, I saw a shadow advancing, an enormous shadow of a man, monstrous and wild, whose face was malevolent, with large shining eyes beneath bushy eyebrows, an unkempt beard, and an evil smile opening over yellow teeth. The Shadow Man advanced; I had an intuition that he would treat me cruelly, and I wanted to run away; I couldn't even succeed in avoiding his menacing gaze, thus escaping the irony of his snigger. Desperate efforts filled me with anxiety without permitting me to accomplish the slightest movement.

"The Shadow Man kept coming forward, becoming gigantic; he was soon very close to me, until we were only separated by the thickness of the wall. He stopped then, and that moment of grace increased my terror. What was he going to do? There was a ladder scaling the wall, and now, carrying a block of stone in his arms, the Shadow Man started climbing that ladder slowly, higher and higher, while I remained there, breathless, my heart squeezed atrociously.

"Then having reached the top, he loomed up, fantastic and immense—I heard his laughter resonating terribly—and, after holding the rock above my head momentarily, the Shadow Man let it go...."

"And then?"

"I uttered a terrible scream, in response to which my mother became accustomed to waking me up, to spare me the horror of the fatal crushing."

"The scene unfolded like that every night?"

"Exactly the same, every night, incessantly, without failing to manifest itself once."

"Always the same?"

"Yes, always the same, and if someone forgot, on hearing my exclamation, to rescue me from the horrible continuation of the nightmare, or if, on occasion, my mother could not get to me quickly enough, the mass of granite came down, accelerating as it fell, increasing in size proportionally; it was about to reach me when, with a supreme howl of distress, I came to, haggard, trembling and covered in sweat."

"Did that go on for a long time?"

"A very long time—until I reached the age of twelve."

"And at that age?"

"There was a fairly long interruption, and I no longer saw the wall, the cause of so much horror, except at rare intervals; the shadow that came to crush me no longer reappeared, but in his place appeared a vague, mute feminine form, which I exhausted myself trying to reach, but who fled, leaving me weary, troubled and discontented by her appearance. I was never able to see her face; she emerged, immaterial and frail, very like those vapors in phantom-like form that were floating out there over the waters this evening. Nowadays, I no longer have those nocturnal visits, and you're here to prevent me from missing the unknown veiled woman too much."

"You loved her, then?"

"I hardly knew her...."

"Come on, be honest!"

"She brightened my dull, sulky youth with a ray of mysterious poetry; and I was certainly sometimes surprised to find myself desiring her presence. So what? Are you going to be jealous of that ancient, entirely fictitious image?"

"Which you haven't forgotten!"

"Silly girl! Remember that you're the present and adorable reality...the other was never anything but a pure phantasmagoria, an illusion, now faded into the past."

Thérèse started laughing. "What, you're taking that joke seriously! I'll be glad never to have any other rival than her!"

Huber Estève added: "Furthermore, I can assure you that I've completely lost sight of her."

Now, in speaking thus, they were both lying.

Contrary to the sentiment of confidence that she

affected, Thérèse, involuntarily influenced by the supernatural appearance in which her lover's story was clad, felt a vague anxiety welling up within her, mingled with hatred directed against the ungraspable creature whose memory Huber retained in his memory without displeasure. Her amorous spirit, candid and violent at the same time, rebelled against the thought of sharing him, even with someone immaterial, and her naïve faith could not tolerated the thought that someone might deceive her, even with the figment of a dream.

As for Huber, he too experienced an instinctive mistrust, but with regard to himself. That confession had sufficed to bring back the old swarm of fears, which had never entirely disappeared, and the anxiety of old. He had, moreover, refrained from admitting that that the last vision dated from only a few hours ago—and how could he know whether, even though the enervating obsession for which he had suffered so much, an apparition terrifying for a child, had become sweeter in the era of puberty, and then disappeared, had not come back, on the occasion of this Breton interlude with his first interlude, reproduced in a form that, if not as dolorous, offered at least as much peril?

Night had fallen: night, the old enemy! She slyly occupied the room, taking her position insidiously, gently establishing her dominion. Successively, she had covered the nooks and crannies with black velvet, had flowed over the creases in the curtains, nestled under the wall-hangings and was now blurring the furniture with a layer of darkness, developing her gray muslins, proceeding with the burial of forms and colors. While the two of them repented, she of her indiscreet curiosity, he of his dangerous confidence, the shadow had slid behind them, a conquering and perfidious traitress. Huber, turning round, perceived that, and shuddered.

Beginning to freshen, the wind forbade them to remain there leaning out of the window, which it was necessary to close. After having lit a candle, the painter sat down in an armchair, and, fixing his eyes on the play of the flame, seemed to absorb himself in that mute contemplation. Nevertheless, as his forehead was striped with little vertical wrinkles and his mouth contracted involuntarily, Thérèse, placing her hands on Estève's shoulders, asked him, in a surprised tone: "What are you thinking about?"

He raised his head, drew her toward him and kissed her without replying, not daring to voice the absurd, crazy and increasing fear that was welling up in him, invading his being, as he fell prey to an indefinable malaise. Hugging her to his breast, he retained her on her knees, glad not to be alone in that moment of crisis.

And yet, what help could Thérèse give him, in that struggle against himself, against that enigmatic part of himself, which constituted a kind of second personality, distinct from the first and always unknown, whose incessant labors retain the anonymity of unconsciousness, and which sometimes reveals itself to others but never to us.

He enlaced his mistress with a feverish grip,

imploring her by that gesture to defend him against the black magic of the unknown, against the spells of the fatal hour, against the smile of the phantom about which he was bound to dream—he was sure of that. But what ironic voice, what spectral whisper, had warned him, at that moment, of the inevitably visitation? Frightened, he tried to fathom the mute obscurity.

Nothing—and Thérèse, who did not understand, relaxed gladly, unsuspecting of his anxiety.

At that moment, he thought he felt his arms coming apart, and then falling gently into empty apace, while the your woman fled, rapidly—so rapidly that before long, he could no longer even make out her imprecise form in the dense shadow.

He wanted to call out to her, but no sound vibrated in the air, which had become heavy.

Then he closed his eyes, and he waited.

II.
Mousmé

How long has he been in this garden, in the shadow of the undulating woods, near the pool whose satin is pleated by the movement of swans? He does not know. Perhaps years have gone by since he climbed over the wall: the strange, semi-transparent wall at the foot of which he can still see himself lying, trembling before the menace of the Shadow Man.

Perhaps!

The environment is familiar to him; he recognizes, in the water, the whiteness of birch-trees mirrored there.

He knows every clump of moss in the hollows of the old trunks fissured by incurable wounds; he inspects the flower-baskets at the edge of which the little Idol sometimes emerges.

How late she is in appearing!

She is often late, like this, and now, retracing the route he has followed many times before, he heads toward the palace, the porphyry steps where a thousand pink granite sphinxes mount guard, and the domes of gold-veined lapis, sparkling among the immaculate terraces.

He climbs the steps—the polished steps, extending to infinity—without appearing to rise up appreciably. When will he reach the bronze doors, whose green patina is shining between the columns of the façade?

Suddenly—he is not astonished by the absence of transition—a rug of pearls opens in the half-light of an immense room holed by innumerable windows, all veiled with mauve blinds. And the little Idol comes forward, gliding rather than walking, over the precious mosaics, through which fugitive gleams and brief glints pass when they are brushed by her dainty, ivory-tinted feet.

Her fingers are laden with rings. Her hair, gathered up on top of her head, forms a high chignon, illuminated by a kind of diadem encrusted with precious stones. She has a slightly arched forehead, her pupils lit up by internal flames, which render the blackness limpid and traversed with fires, like a gem. Her eyelids, drowned in bistre, frame orbs magnified by milky sclerotics. Her small nose with sensual nostrils, her ember-red mouth and, above all, the incomparable transparency of a mat complexion, so warmly colored that it seems luminous, lend her the appearance of a daughter of the Orient.

Now, because she evokes within him the memory of the finely-carved figurines that he admired one feast-day in the dwelling of the Maharajah of Sahrou, he calls her Mousmé.[6]

Musical instruments are audible in the painter's head, and a metronome in his temples regulates the cadence. Very faintly, tunes sound, emanating from distant concerts, played by sad, gentle and frail instruments. But that melody is not only in his ears! He can see it, and it from the Lover that it is disengaged. He can perceive, surely, the trills of her smile, the arpeggios of her gaze, the song of her visage, the accompaniment of the decorated veils that traverse, in an incessantly recalled leitmotiv, a broad sapphire-blue belt.

The instruments play, and their modulations vary in accordance with the iridescence of fabrics, to which the movements of the little Idol thus impart a scale of nuances and fugitive sounds, each of her attitudes creating an entire poem of light and harmony. The fris-

---

6. It is extremely unlikely that Danville knew of the existence of Vincent van Gogh's painting "La Mousmé," painted in 1888, which is nowadays the best-known referent of this word; Danville almost certainly appropriated it from the same source as van Gogh: Pierre Loti's novel *Madame Chrysanthème* (1887), although it is employed there as a trivial noun to refer to a Japanese girl. The "Sahrou" to which reference is made in respect of a hypothetical "Maharajah" is probably Sahoro in Japan, and the title an eccentric adaptation.

sons of the silk have the timbre of dolorous weeping violins, with which the Aeolian susurrus of harps is combined in more somber passages. A necklace of sequins, speckled with random flashes, resonates after the fashion of silvery trumpets. Muslin scarves spread out in the plaints of oboes, and on the ankles and the wrists that they circle, bracelets sound like timpani or tambourines.

Alas, as She approaches, the colors blur and the sounds evaporate, with the result that Mousmé is reduced, in proximity to Huber, to an ungraspable mist, a thin shadow, in which only the onyx of her eyes and the garnet of her lips remain, faintly perceptible, half-effaced upon the gray weave.

In spite of her transformation, however, a magnificent, intoxicating charm invests the image, like those admirable ancient pastels whose tones are extinct, whose vigor dead, but which nevertheless retain an indelible beauty.

The painter admires her and then begins to murmur ironically—is he waking up?—"Dreams! Lies!"

Now, although the red tint of the phantasmal lips does not stir, he hears: "My friend, Mousmé is not a deceptive dream; if the palace she inhabits is thought, reflect that you could not have accorded her any other shelter, for this one is common to all existent realities."

"A sad palace, from which you never emerge! A cloister that keeps you eternally imprisoned!"

"And why?"

"Because you only exist through me."

She laughs prettily, which causes Huber to shiver, and exclaims, in the course of a joyful trill: "Conceited and presumptuous! Oh, you really are a man, are you not? And how, if you please, do I only exist through you?"

"Well," he replies, shaken, "if I no longer wanted to think about Mousmé, Mousmé would cease to exist."

"Is that true?"

"It's at least logical."

"Undoubtedly! Would you dare, however, to claim that you have not been tempted not to think about Mousmé any longer?"

"I've tried, I admit."

"And what happened?"

"I didn't succeed, I similarly admit."

"What conclusion do you draw?"

"None," he replies, after some hesitation.

"You bad faith is evident, my dear Estève; nevertheless, I shall pass on, and ask you, in the second place, in what way I differ, so far as you are concerned, from a reality?"

Huber does not reply. He no longer knows whether he is hallucinating or dreaming, and does not want to know, for the voluptuous, enveloping caress of the Lover has become urgent, and it no longer seems to him that she is unreal. Under the red deluge of kisses, his entire being, whipped and overstimulated by bitter, intense desire, is breathless, frightened, and hectically vibrant.

From his loins to the nape of his neck, a stream of

boiling lead is drilling into his marrow, and while he cries out a supreme: "Forgive me…forgive me for having doubted you, Mousmé, I love you!" the little Idol vanishes, with a mocking: "Until tomorrow!"

Estève chokes back a cry of rage.

As if their hinges have rusted, the shutters of his eyelids are difficult to raise. The painter's soul, disappointed, amply saturated with bitterness, searches the banal, empty room, poor lit by a wan pre-dawn light.

Thérèse is still asleep; the rhythm of her respiration and the distant tumult of the waves, breaking at regular intervals on the rocks and beaches, barely reach Huber's brain. Gradually, however, those sounds are magnified and combined, but without troubling a bewildered, haggard semi-somnolence, which renders almost painful the consciousness of a parade of involuntary and derisory delusions before the void, of chimeras forged by himself, and perhaps also the regret of no longer being the happy plaything amusing the enchantress issued from an Imaginary era; over the tapestry of confused and sad perceptions, exasperating a sensibility quick to suffer, crazy fears are sketched, born of the strangeness of the sensations received, unhealthily denatured.

Estève would like to move, to escape by means of action, by means of flight, the evil influence of the idea that sketches itself all too precisely; now, paralyzing rivets of impotence immobilize his limbs, all the muscles of his body seeming to contract in vain. He can scarcely take account of the position of his body, which dematerializes, effaces itself, vanishes, and goes away: very far away, beyond the gray, wide, immeasurable spaces.

Close to him, by contrast, an indecisive rumor sometimes becomes clearer; it is a buzz of hornets, punctuated by brief roars, claps of thunder; where is it coming from? Thérèse—the sea! And those two images combine, confused into a single one, absurd and bizarre, which imposes itself by virtue of that very fact, victoriously combating the reason that protests.

Has not his being sunk in the ocean of heavy materiality, entangled therein? The purr of the waves, the woman's sighs, now augmenting in intensity, shaking—with what force!—his eardrum like the enervating rumble of some immense machine, which he cannot see, but which he can divine, which has certainly drawn him into its turbulent mass, which is finally crushing him in its embrace; for—and this is real, atrociously real!—is he not sinking further into those heavy waves, is he not, this time, being crushed by the soft and stifling gears?

He is breathless; his throat is tight, as if gripped by a pitiless vice. The horrible oppression!

…And his heart mingles its beating with that of the waves, and the enormous, anguishing breath of the woman, exaggerating now the periodic, irresistible surge of that sonorous flux, the vibrations of each assault of which pound his miserable head, so hot that one might think it fill of blazing coals, indescribably.

While in that fantastic Inferno, undergoing abominable tortures, superhuman damnations, he remains panting, exhausted, but nevertheless extending his crucified cerebration in a supreme effort, to offer his tortures as a propitiatory holocaust to the divine Lover—and now, beneath his fluttering eyelids, the little Idol with the enigmatic and smiling lips appears, radiant, in a lily-white paradisal dazzle, resplendent, utterly pure.

Mousmé! It's Mousme!

And the garden of dreams, and the pool whose satin is creased by the gliding of swans, and the wall of crystal, and the palace with domes of lapis! Musical instruments playing, and Mousmé!

The Gehenna in which clenched teeth are still grinding is succeeded for Huber by the enchantment of incomparable delights, of the warm joy that only the presence of the Lover confers upon him.

Gold! Gold in liquid rays! Gold, everywhere! A seething of roseate gold, blond gold, bright gold, transparent, airy and sparkling, spreads its light, its opalescence, its reflections of changing gauze laminated with metal; and within that radiance of ideal hues, surging forth with the coralline Dawn, the mystical figure of the little Idol, which symbolizes now for the wounded man both the eternal victory of radiant consoling Daylight over the Darkness of evil, and the healing power of Love, which dissipates horrible suffering. Thus it provokes in him the spontaneous gush of a hymn of adoration and gratitude, and the ecstatic babbling of words of delight, truly sincere by virtue of being dictated, by physical recognition, the only strength, and by the poignant memory of the recent crisis, and finally by the infinite enjoyment that accompanies any deliverance.

"Forgive me, Mousmé! Mousmé, I love you! For a long time, in the night, you have come; you have come and I have wanted, stupidly, to know the secret of your essence, as if it were permitted for mortals to penetrate the nature of divinities, the mystery of their designs. You depart, leaving the needle of desire fixed in my heart, and also the regret of having offended your sphinx-like majesty. Now, you have deigned to come back, to liberate me, when I was struggling, a prisoner in the abysms of a Tartarus of stupefying dolor; you have deigned to come back—oh, don't leave me again!

"I no longer want to know. No. And even if you were the daughter of my thought, and even if you named yourself an illusion or a lie, I would gladly commit the supreme incest, I would abandon myself to the deceptive mirage. Don't take offense at that language!— because, you see, I don't know what is dream and what is reality, and I know that we're the eternal dupes of appearances.

"My reason takes fright before those problems, remains impotent to search, behind the mobile cloud of phenomena, for first causes, constant relationships— the truth, in sum; and I sense that in contemplating you I become parallel to a man who, being subject to vertigo, would willingly lean over a gulf. What does it matter to me whether I fall into it…with you? Perhaps a destiny worse than death awaits me there; I shall no longer resist it.

"Whatever you are, Mousmé, it is through you and you alone that I want to live! Mousmé, I love you; can you forgive me?"

Blackness darkens the mind of the painter, who is soon resting in the unconsciousness of sleep.

Thérèse, awakened a few moments ago, has listened in fear to Estève's plea, and begins to weep silently. Seemingly replying to her, the bounding waves moan in the distance, making a great racket, on the matinal beaches caressed by the sun.

III.
The Mistress and the Lover

On the horizon, clad in blur-tinted mists, fleecy woods extend; fields of buckwheat stretch out their russet rectangles beneath the sunlight, toward the meadows where lowing cattle are grazing, belonging to the farm whose low dry-stone walls rise up, pocked with narrow loopholes, with its thatched roofs, between hayricks the color of rust, not far from the stream overhung by beeches; trembling poplars shade the washerwomen whose head-dresses spangle the reed-edged waters with ceruse flashes.

Estève's brush rapidly places a few strokes on the canvas, and the landscape grows, becomes clearer, and is slowly animated; the background retreats, the foreground is displayed in richer, more colorful and more vigorous detail; emerging from the vagueness of the sketch, the characters begin to come to life. In the surroundings there is a sovereign moist warmth, which would be suffocating without the brief, enervating gusts of wind blowing from the sea, harbingers of an imminent storm. Above the withered and desiccated grass at the edge of the road, the overheated air undulates and quivers, and the crickets screech noisily.

The painter is working feverishly, full of verve, taking careful note of all the shades and the tones and their nuances; he is unaware of the ambient temperature, which turns Thérèse's cheeks pink, dapples the top of her forehead with pearly droplets, and imparts a vague numbness to her entire being.

Like a flock of ospreys, which only daylight suffices to chase away, the dark ideas have disappeared from her mind; for, influenced without knowing it by the healthy gaiety of the striking and joyful symphony of light emanating from the surroundings, the young woman is reassured in seeing Huber at work, courageously and delightedly, so very different from the terrifying illuminate glimpsed that morning in the sadness of an evil awakening; so she has abandoned herself to a renewal of confidence.

She is so astonished by such a transformation, such a contrast, that she fears that she might have been the dupe of some deceptive vision, which might have troubled her awakening, by showing her fears that are doubtless imaginary realized. She is unaware of the incessant modifications by which our thoughts are afflicted, by virtue of their very combination, either, according to circumstance, by the state of mind that constitutes our momentary personality, or by the multiple and so very various sensations by which our being is charged under external influences, ineptly hiding the possibility of the alternation in a single individual of several incarnations—so different from one another that Estève, for example, could successively represent the Lover of Mousmé, the Artist, the lover of Thérèse, and the affable Man of the World: the only one known to casual acquaintances.

Unable, as yet, to differentiate these composite entities, the simple soul of the young woman models itself on the temporary sentiment of the moment, obtaining a great placid pleasure from watching Huber at work, enjoying the splendid afternoon sunlight, going as far as to accuse of being an ill-founded anxiety the thrill of fear procured for her by the memory of the troubling scene of the morning.

A short distance away, two little girls, lying on their backs on a grassy bank, are chatting in the singsong voices with the soft and harmonious accents particular to the region, which one might imagine to be inspired by the plaint that modulates the waves on silent nights. Sometimes, too, bursts of youthful laughter punctuate the dialogues with their shrill notes, like an intense vibration of pure metal. They chatter away, amused by trivia, insouciant, while both attached by long cords brushing the ground and retained by pegs driven into the ground to the sheep they are guarding, grazing the grass whose greenness had almost been reduced to yellow, so dry is it.

While Huber, turning his head slightly, is wiping his brushes, he perceives the little peasants, and immediately, abandoning the painting in progress, attempts to capture on a wooden panel the impish physiognomy of one of the suntanned children, whose swarthy laughing face, surrounded by a tousled nimbus of wrack-brown hair, appears in the half-light created by the shadow of her broad-brimmed straw hat like a pretty medallion of pale bronze, which Life has covered with a luminous patina, a warm glaze of mauve and orange.

How, for that face, has another substituted itself, beneath the constructive charcoal of the sketch?

In spite of the humidity of the stormy afternoon, Huber felt an icy wind pass over his face, a frosty breath that chilled him all the way to the marrow of his bones. The charcoal fell from his fearful fingers— from the fingers that had drawn that!

It seemed to him that he had been transported into a world of mysteries, and the great enigma of the supernatural posed itself to his thoughts, where alarm and doubt were germinating. If his hand was no longer obedient to him, who, then, had guided it in that fashion, in order to realize precisely the constant object of his preoccupations, that obsessive, desirable phantom, in order that it should trace the perfect effigy of amiable resemblance, the exact portrait of the little Idol?

With a noise similar to the muffled crackle of powerful musketry, the thunder commenced growling dully, and its echoes reverberated through the air, running across the vast plains of the sky, repeating the multiple resonances of the frightful strokes of a gong to infinity.

As the sky suddenly darkened, Huber almost expected a miracle. Nothing happened, but he distinctly heard Mousmé's words resonating within him, the strange words to which he had been unable to reply: "I ask you," she said, "in what way I differ from a reality?"

And on the white wood, the eyes of the strange silhouette darkened, the nostrils attempting to palpitate, while the corners of the mouth rose up like two pink wings, sarcastic and mocking.

And Estève thought: *A living model certainly couldn't have inspired me any more, and yet, she wasn't there. She's never been there....*

A *who can tell?* stopped him. And that interrogation, he was sure of not having proffered, for he had not recognized the sound of his own voice.

Large drops of water, anticipating the bulk of the inundation, fell just in time to put an end to the confusion that was beginning to take possession of the painter. The increasing abundance of the rain forced him to regain a footing in the real, in order to ward off more urgent material threats. It was necessary to think about running for some nearby shelter, but the nearest village, as well as the hotel where Estève was staying, was some distance away.

One of the little shepherdesses then pointed to the windmill of Roche-Milan, whose ancient framework was perceptible close by, standing on a rocky outcrop, its sails profiling an abridgement of a somber St. Andrew's cross against a gray silk background formed by the collapse of the clouds. Beside it, low down, crushed beneath a thatched roof, subsiding in places and patched up like a pauper's coat, a small house appeared, like a little old woman humbly crouching next to her master, the ancient edifice whose framework reared up masterfully, still solid in spite of the assaults off the weather, the planking disjointed by storm winds and the worm-eaten appearance of its shaky sails.

Thérèse and Huber arrived at a run at the low door of the building and, having opened it, went into a room with an earthen floor: the "living room" in which people cooked, ate and slept. An old man was sitting by the fireside. Faggots were burning in the hearth beneath a large pot suspended from a hook, and the gold, blue and red flames of the fire were varnishing the soot of the vessel with warm tones, contrasting in their richness with the miserable aspect of everything else. Reflections rendered luminous by the semi-darkness reigning in the room went forth to caress the woodwork of the bed and the cupboards with fugitive gleams; bronze utensils shone brightly among them.

The old man was the former captain of a coaster, as was sufficiently indicated by the brick-red color of his face, communicated by long hauls in the wind and the sun. He hastened to bring his unexpected guests chairs, excusing his clumsiness by his poor eyesight. And indeed, in front of his dull eyes, starred with steel blue, cataracts extended a veil that was already opaque, misting the transparency of his weak gaze.

At that moment, a terrible crack rent the air, and torrents of water sprang forth, unleashed, inundating the area, striking the narrow windows forcefully. Lightning flashes were succeeding one another rapidly now, in the din of uninterrupted rolls of thunder. At each dazzling streak, the fantastic shadow of the windmill stood out clearly against a background of intense white light, tinted with violet.

Impressed by the moving spectacle, the painter and his mistress maintained silence; only the mariner proffered sententious appreciations in a muted voice, which emerged from his toothless mouth in short bursts: "The poor wheat-fields were so dry…. It's that accursed souwesterly wind…. I said as much this morning…. You could have offered me gold but I wouldn't even have wanted to take a boat across the bay…not even as far as the mud of Boudineaux. At this hour, the fellows that go out are crazy…it's necessary, all the same, to risk one's life for a few wretched fish…."

Soon, however, Huber no longer heard the quavering chant; his previous thoughts, the obsessive thoughts, rushed once again to assault his reason. His mind focused on the troubling problem posed by Mousmé, without being able to turn away from it, and with the same fatality that draws a magnetized needle toward a constant point.

What, then, was the true, the real? What conditions of human existence imposed certainty? Ill-prepared for such doubts, his slender baggage of philosophy reduced to the givens of common sense, Estève ran into difficulties there that he had not expected. He was frightened by his inability to find arguments capable of compelling his immediate conviction. And yet, far from deterring him, that resistance further sharpened his desire. On seeing the landscape suddenly illuminated, and then falling back into a half-light contrasted with the broad daylight in which he had been working, and considering the infinite variation of shades, he formulated elementary reservations regarding the absolute value of the information provided by observation of the external world.

In any case, did he not know that his painter's vision differed from that of the vulgar, since he was able to perceive blues, violets, and pinks where the ignorant could only distinguish uniform gray or brown colorations? Did not the instability of forms and colors that he observed, and the further deceptions of perspective, of which he made facile quotidian use, demonstrate the fact, which he had already sensed confusedly without having penetrated its importance, that the testimony of the senses is often illusory and is not, in consequence, irrefutable? From where do we obtain our knowledge of things, if not solely through our senses?

That observation rendered him uneasy. How did those deductions follow one another in such logical connection? He did not recognize the ideas as his own, could not admit that he had given birth to them. It appeared to him that a new personality had been born in his soul, lifting up a veil of errors in whose shelter he had thus far lived unawares, and it was with a surprise extending almost to terror that he listened to that newcomer, that stranger born, so to speak, of himself.

Since the disquieting confidence that had escaped him the previous evening, almost unwittingly, resuscitating the moribund host of memories of old, the painter had been struggling desperately against the invasive tide of Mystery, the Unknown and the Inexplicable that had arrived to turn his being upside down. His reason vaguely perceived the inanity of the phantoms agitating around him. Nevertheless, when the face of Mousmé, the conversation with the little Idol, and the words spoken a little while ago on the subject of the portrait—and he had definitely heard them!—returned to Estève's mind, the unfortunate, shaken by the positive affirmation of that remembrance, and especially by the surprising intensity in which the various images were clad, was gripped by doubt.

Had not that suspicion acquired substance within himself? Had not a part of his soul appointed itself the advocate of that troubling cause? Huber, carried away by the whirlwind of contradictory ideas struggling in his mind, experienced the anguish of a swimmer who has lost his footing and no longer feels himself the master of directing his movements, so irresistible is the violence of the currents disputing his possession.

In that moment of distress, on the point of sinking— and into such dangerous abysms!—he suddenly thought of Thérèse; a flame of hope seared him. However, even though he fought against it, the strange figure of Mousmé, the mysterious side of the adventure, attracted him invincibly. The image of Thérèse was insufficient to vanquish the obsession, which, deep within him, he began to desire to be complete, durable and entirely realized, in spite of taking account of the irremediable peril that the advent of such a desire created, and perhaps even because he had that notion of danger, from which emanated a kind of mental vertigo, drawing him into the gulf.

An ultimate effort of his reason nevertheless overcame those deadly oscillations, attempting to reestablish equilibrium by bearing the painter toward his mistress. He fixed his attention upon her with a dolorous persistence, which was a kind of supplicant appeal, a supreme attempt of defense against the dear Enemy, the Lover. It was an appeal more instinctive than willed, a platonic aspiration, for the artist had already accorded victory to Mousmé in beginning to desire feverishly, in opposition to himself, that Thérèse would not understand the reason for his intense gaze.

Nevertheless, the young woman, before those haggard, frightened eyes, abruptly remembered what had been said the previous evening, and the scene that morning that had disturbed her so much; and, by virtue of an intuition generated by those memories, she almost divined Huber's anguish. Her heart contracted, as if at the announcement of an unforeseen misfortune, when she saw her vague dreads thus take form, her scattered suspicions coming together rapidly to form a bundle, of which the various incidents that had led to that point formed the links: a conviction, she now knew, that would trouble her permanently. So, the Other, the Rival that she still did not know, had loomed up between them once again! Her lover's attitude was equivalent, in that regard, to the clearest of confessions.

As well as being wounded in her amour, she felt afflicted in her self-esteem. Why had Huber lied to her, hidden the truth from her, when she had always shown herself to be full of affectionate confidence to him? He had played a part with her, and now, once again, the belated revelation that his gaze contained was incomplete. Could she, in fact, have understood what that mute supplication signified, if she had not, unknown to him, been a witness to his dream?

Thérèse's anguish was further increased by her impotence. What could she do against that fictitious being issued from her lover's imagination, who had succeeded in dominating him in spite of his own efforts? Must she, on the other hand, resign herself to abandoning all hope, enclosing herself in the indifferent disdain, the coldness, that would avenge the insult offered to the candor of her love?

She had already resigned herself to the latter course when, just as she turned her head away, she stopped. What, then, had prevented her from accomplishing the liberating movement, retaining her in her desire to return to frankness?

She perceived then that the voice of passion had risen up within her, louder than that of pride. However despicable Huber had become, she could not stop loving him. All of her flesh spoke to her, more imperiously than her mind; her body vibrated with ancient caresses as the idea of losing him.

At that protest of her entire being, Thérèse did not feel that she had the strength to move on.

But how could she reconquer her beloved? If she had been alone with him, she could have rapidly accumulated convincing proofs, sure arguments to make him renounce that vain pursuit of a chimera. Here, in this strange environment, in the company the old man with the pale eyes, who was talking about unknown countries and Death, she did not now how to act to extract Huber from his folly.

He was still gazing at her, with an already-disquieting expression of emptiness, of vagueness, of the beyond, which was unfamiliar to her, and which increased her fear.

Run away, as quickly as possible!

That idea imposed itself upon her mind as the only possible solution, for the moment. In any case, the storm was moving away; it was no longer raining, and they could hear once again the grating of the millstones grinding the wheat, while the black sails of he old windmill launched themselves in grandiose flight, whose regular subsequent fall veiled all the windows of the little cottage simultaneously with a curtain of shadow.

Now, just as one employs frowns of annoyance and severe expressions with little children, Thérèse suppressed her tenderness and thought it appropriate to put on a harsh mask, to adopt a curt and authoritarian tone in order to speak to her lover.

"What's the matter with you?" she said, rapidly, in a low voice. "You look ridiculous, staring at me like that, with that distraught expression. Come on! There's no need for us to stay here any longer. Let's go!"

They bade farewell to the old captain, and quit the hovel in which, unknown to their host and almost to themselves, the crucial scene of that entirely psychic drama had been played, the action of which passed in thoughts and associations of ideas, in deductions and not in gestures.

The few words pronounced by Thérèse, and in that rude tone, insignificant in themselves, had impressed Huber forcefully by virtue of their unaccustomed brutality. Thanks to the disturbance he was experiencing, they soon took on the importance of a considerable event; the painter was alarmed by no longer finding the benevolent, affectionate and submissive young woman that he knew. That determined abruptness, masking a real generosity, made him believe in a defection by his mistress.

Thérèse no longer loved him!

He accompanied her mechanically, marching like a sleepwalker. He did not see the blond sun smiling over the soothing sea, nor the sparkling waves bounding beneath that caress like a troop of young fawns, nor the pink beaches over which the foam of the roaring waves was breaking. Nor did he see the tears that Thérèse was having difficulty retaining behind her eyelids, or that her breast was stirred by muffled sobs, or that her gait was precipitate, in order that she would not tremble.

Through the golden gorse and the heather pearled by brilliant droplets he went, behind her, unconscious of the magnificence of the surroundings, wounded by the incessant bite of despairing thoughts.

Thérèse no longer loved him!

That illogical deduction, legitimated for him solely by the fact of the peevish tone with which the young woman had replied to his heartsick plea, had become a certainty, fortified, while it persisted in the painter's soul, by a rampart of adventitious ideas: a certainty soon unshakable, for it came at a moment when Huber's mind, weary of fatiguing indecision, was in search of a fixed point on which it could rest—and besides, the desire that he had not dared to formulate was thus realized.

From the very accomplishment of that secret desire, however, emanated, for the artist, an insidious and perfidious dolor, which he had not anticipated; he certainly had not thought that Thérèse loved him so little, that she could so rapidly detach herself from him, recovering herself. In vain he repeated that it was necessary to congratulate himself on a solution that permitted him to belong, without any scruple, entirely to Mousmé; he could not succeed—so complex is the host of contrary sentiments that share the brain of an individual!—in dissipating the bad feeling that the event, in spite of being desired, now caused him, procuring him nevertheless a resentful, unforeseen and painful astonishment.

Then, it seemed to him that a flood of darkness gradually invaded his heart, without his being able to struggle against that invasion, which inundated him with blackness, stifled his last plaints and regrets under a mattress of opaque mists, insurmountable to his former tendencies of affection.

He felt that curtain of indifference darken progressively, thickening the veil of cold fog, which soon completely hid all the happiness of a common past, all the sympathetic inclinations still subsisting for Thérèse, and even the very memory of that past. When nothing any longer remained of it, a reaction set in, and from the melancholy suffering that it provoked, Huber passed without transition to a wild, new, hitherto unknown delight.

An intense sensation of wellbeing invaded him entirely.

Thérèse was walking close by. The play of the light in her ashen hair animated her forehead, imperceptibly creased, with a radiant life. Her eyes, moist with repressed tears, borrowed from that humid gleam a singular, troubling profundity; and, graceful, with a perfect harmony of forms, her silhouette was outlined on the edge of the cliff, her skirts fluttering in the breeze, borrowing from the serenity of the superb décor the necessary complement also to display a real and splendid symbol of Youth and Life.

Even the painter in Huber did not quiver, any more than the lover, before that apparition.

The mistress had had her day.

Alone, and victorious, the mysterious Lover, the dear little Idol, was evoked, brought closer to her adorer by the decline of the daylight—for the night was advancing, propitious to supernatural devotions.

IV.

"Do not believe that I fear seeing my spirit flee through the dark doors of cruel death."

(Omar Khayyam)

A day in September, all in shades of gray, beneath a leaden dome.

Huber had recognized the impossibility of working and, alone in his studio, sprawling rather than sitting on the divan, he was amusing himself in following the capricious play of opaline smoke. His thoughts were floating like the undulating blue ribbons, delightfully languid, unfurling a tenuous train of thin, fragile and rapidly-dissipated images.

Without anything having given rise to the expectation, the painter had abruptly escaped the anguishing and sweet obsession to which, for him, the dream of the Breton heaths had given rise. Mousmé had not accompanied him in his return, and no longer reappeared here. No dream persisted as the equal of the real, and no recurrence of the strange vision had occurred; the cherished image had vanished.

Still influenced by the recent memory of his crisis, Huber had thought about all the things that he could not explain, astonished to have believed, seriously, in the phantasmagoria of such an adventure, and had then experienced ill-concealed regret that it had come to an end so soon.

After having lived every night in a fictitious world, possessed an impeccable and triumphant Lover, he could not be content only with existent material things, and began confusedly to desire the return of a similar doubling of his life, while recognizing willingly enough, at present, that he had duped himself, in the sense that Mousmé only owed her existence, as he had initially thought, to his own imagination. For a time, however, he had mistaken the little Idol for a creature acting spontaneously, constituted by an essence other than himself, endowed with sentiments that belonged entirely to her. To be sure, he had loved her as much as any carnal creature, and not as a virtual, nonexistent individual.

Swaying between the data furnished to the painter by his memory, tending to represent Mousmé as possessed of a certain reality, and the reasoning of his logic, which demonstrated the unfounded nature of such a conception, Huber hesitated to reach a conclusion, running into irreconcilable arguments, but offering so much plausibility on the one hand, and so much common sense on the other, that he could not decide to settle the question in favor of either hypothesis.

Thus far, the change of environment, the various occupations linked to his return to Paris, the relationships resumed, and many other multiple causes of the same sort, had distracted to painter's soul from any idea of the same kind as those that had just agitated him; perhaps, too, they had chased away the obsessive image that he called Mousmé. Now those thoughts presented themselves again, doubtless brought back by the particular mental disposition in which the artist found himself that afternoon: the nonchalance and voluntary laziness into which he had relaxed; the absence of urgent preoccupations.

Undoubtedly, during their sojourn in that part of ourselves of which we are ignorant, which elaborates slow projects of which we are unaware, associations fertile in the unexpected had acquired a new force thanks to that labor of unconscious aggregation, inoffensive to begin with, but nevertheless just as dangerous as the old obsession. The latter, in fact, did not reappear, but in its place the desire surged forth in Huber, still confused, for its reproduction, accompanied by its cortege of desirable hallucinations.

For after all, the artist concluded, as he terminated a critical review of the objections regarding Mousmé, *the real problem isn't contained in these almost metaphysical considerations, which exhaust me in turning over all their angles, pointlessly, as I don't have the science necessary to envisage them competently and discover some luminous indication of truth therein; it's necessary for me to stick to the solid terrain of undeni-*

able facts, sensed and perceived, experienced sensa-
tions, manifest phenomena, without attempting vainly
to interpret them. Returning to that point of view, the
only one at which its appropriate to place myself in
order to obtain a practical indication as well as a
prompt solution, the question that I'm led to ask myself
is no longer "Does Mousmé have a real existence or
not? Was I witness to an astral projection, descended
from the perispirit,[7] or the visitation of a fluid, reincar-
nate soul, possessed by a succubus or simply duped by
a hallucination?" No, what's important to me is simply
the question of whether or not I was happy during that
mysterious period.

Well, I confess frankly that I knew then, for the first
time, passion in its full intensity, that I was sincerely
in love. What does it matter if that love was addressed
to a Chimera? I have, at least, obtained the supreme
happiness....

As Huber had adopted as a rule of life an intelligent Epicureanism, never letting an opportunity for
possible pleasures pass, so as to reduce necessary evils
to a minimum, while limiting those joys in terms of the
dolors that might ensue therefrom, he naturally found
himself led, by that manner of habitual action, to wish
for the reproduction of the recent state of affairs—
the return of Mousmé—since he judged her capable
of making him happy. He did not perceive, or did not

---

7. "Perispirit" is a term coined by Allen Kardec, the principal founder
of the French school of "spiritism"; it refers to a hypothetical conduit
connecting the spirit to the perceptions of the brain, imagined as a body
analogous to the pineal "gland" in Descartes' model of the mind.

want to perceive, the danger there was in separating himself from normality, in seeking the disequilibrium by virtue of which that separation of the spirit into two separate existences would be procured.

However, would not the affection—or rather jealousy—of Thérèse, still alert to the memory of the events that had occurred out there, constitute an obstacle difficult to overcome? The artist gave himself the excuse that no legal convention created reciprocal duties for them. They were only linked by mutual agreement, and thus remained free to separate if disagreements arose. Furthermore, if he could not hide it, what sin was he committing? He was only deceiving her slightly, after all, and, so far as the world was concerned, in an implausible fashion, not giving grounds, by virtue of that fact, for any criticism, however ardently ill-intentioned it might be.

Another barrier loomed up almost immediately between Huber and his goal, strongly desired for the moment. What, in fact, could he do to evoke the return of the little Idol? His will-power alone was impotent to create the Mousmé of his dreams.

An immense discouragement invaded him; then, bracing himself against that suddenly-manifest obstacle, he acquired a more powerful reaction therefrom; his irritation served to increase the intensity of the initially-hesitant desire, which was reinforced thereby, and acquired a force equivalent to the resistance the painter encountered.

Straight away, he tried to represent the little Idol

to himself, as he contemplated her when he appeared in the immense hall with the innumerable windows veiled by mauve blinds, in the hall paved with precious mosaics that reflected the ivory of her dainty feet, her fingers laden with rings, in the hall of the palace with the porphyry perron, guarded by a thousand pink granite sphinxes, the palace whose domes of gold-veined lapis sparkled amid the immaculate terraces.

In vain.

He exhausted himself in frustration, trying to recover the cherished features; details sometimes emerged from the shroud of forgetfulness, only to sink back into it immediately; and the whole—the charming face, the delicate body, the slender limbs—remained unperceived, in spite of his efforts.

The painter abruptly got up from the divan where, with his eyes closed and his head laid back on the cushions, he had attempted the impossible resurrection, and marched back and forth in the studio, with long strides, his heart gripped by an indescribable sadness and his forehead burning with a sudden fever. He would have liked to scream with all his might, to howl his despair at the calm and inanimate objects surrounding him, thus to kill his grief by brutal action. No sound emerged from his contracted throat, as if his jaws were being held shut by some powerful vice. He felt his eyelids bitten by an acrid sensation, a sudden drying up of his tears. He would have liked to shed them, to extinguish with that benevolent dew the fire of anguish that was torturing him, but only the bitterness of the resorbed tears persisted.

Atrocious suffering!

In a surge of faith, attaining the transports of believers, he invoked Mousmé, the cruel absentee, imploring her with an eloquent supplication, an emotional prayer, to help him, as she had done before, one sad morning when he was suffering in the same fashion.

He became a child again, in order to pray better.

Then, the silence only being punctuated by the rhythmic tick of an old clock, untroubled by the expected murmur, space not revealing the ideal form so desperately desired, Huber blasphemed, rejected his idol with a terrible hatred, an overflow of outrage so passionate that there was still love in it.

One of his glances having encountered, then, a sketch of a woman's head hanging on the wall among other studies, he remembered, by a rapid connection of ideas, the portrait of Mousmé dashed off so curiously by the sea, and set about trying to find it among the canvases and panels brought back from Brittany, which, after his return, had remained stacked in a corner, without any further sorting.

An old church appeared first, then a series of sketches made at dusk: red or golden skies, swept by violet clouds, overhanging sumptuous seas, reverberating those superb glories, the reflections sometimes attenuated by the nascent shadows. The windmill of the Roche-Milan presented itself in its turn.

Gripped once again by the magic of remembrance,

rendered more forceful for having been provoked by the sight of that sketch, the association of the important scene taking him back to it, the painter stopped turning over the canvases, and relived the entire silent drama played out on that stormy evening in the hovel shaken by thunderclaps, in front of the half-blind former mariner.

Insensibly, his mind lent itself to that invasion by memory, which favored, by reconstituting the anterior decor, with the partial aid of the material representation furnished by the picture, the possible return of the contemporary states of mind, without Huber being aware of it.

It was thus that, having finally discovered the face rapidly sketched in charcoal that day, the artist, without a stir of anger, was gripped instead by a troubling emotion, compounded out of the almost religious adoration of a devotee, repentance of the sacrilege he had committed, and the tenderness and ecstatic joy occasioned by the return of the little Idol.

With a naïve and passionate gesture, the painter glued his mouth to the colored wood.

At that moment, he perceived with his lips a slightly insipid, very gentle sensation by which he was surprised, but the provenance of which he could not immediately determine.

Before sorting through the studies painted in the course of his trip, he had, with a mechanical movement, taken a cigarette from the bowl set on the credenza at the foot of which they were leaning. There was opiated tobacco there, rolled in the leaves of nenuphar lilies, which he had kept from a voyage to India.

He continued smoking, while gazing amorously at the visage, barely sketched, of the recovered Lover.

Eventually, by insensible degrees, the beloved face seemed to come to life, and Huber was watching the transformation take place, ecstatically, when, after the fashion of an imperious and mournful knell, the words resonated within him that he had pronounced, in the fashion of a solemn oath, assuring Musmé that it was through her alone, and for her alone, that he lived.

He had perjured himself....

In his brain, darkened by opium fumes, a conviction was born: that it was to the transgression of his promise that he had to attribute the long absence of the little Idol.

The mute image widened her onyx eyes, and appeared to say yes.

Huber bowed his head.

He did not implore forgiveness but wanted to die.

A voice, which he recognized, whispered in his ear....

The painter dropped the panel then, because Mousmé rose up before him, dazzling, ornamented like a goddess, with a nimbus of pale light. She was smiling.

He thanked her, glad in the depths of his soul that she had chosen a slow death for him, the pain of which would be effaced by her kisses; and the red lips of the little Idol drank the soul of the painter through his own mouth, by way of recompense.

Then, she made an imperious gesture, which caused her bracelets to rattle: a commanding gesture that brooked no delay.

Huber obeyed.

His eyes riveted to those of the Lover, his entire being drowned by an indescribable voluptuousness, he slowly plunged the platinum needle into his palpitating, joyful flesh.

Mousmé smiled again.

The painter then completed his first injection of morphine.

THE STOLEN HEART

No preliminary understanding, and no special circumstance had guided us, so far as I know, on that memorable evening when we found ourselves assembled at Ourosoff's, a few intimate friends chatting there, in the half-light of the already darkened smoking-room. It was time to take tea; the water was purring in the brass samovar, the wines and liqueurs were strung out in a multicolored scale gleaming like precious stones; cigarette smoke was adding an azure tint to the atmosphere.

The prince's attitude seemed singular to me. In contrast to his customary phlegm, he seemed agitated; his tall, supple and elegant frame, molded in a dark frock-coat, was silhouetted by frequent comings and goings; his face, of an almost morbid dullness, was even paler than usual. Sudden frissons ran over it, furrowing the polite mask with brief wrinkled, which died away at the corners of his contracted lips. In his eyes, ordinarily gray, not very bright and tinted with old blue, fugitive gleams lit up, especially when Ourousoff, in the course of his feverish prowling, stopped in front of an old item of furniture: a very curious piece in the

Renaissance style. He considered it at length, his gaze then taking on a fixity that astonished us all.

Although surprised by that change in behavior, accustomed as we were to the abrupt shifts of the Slav temperament, whose atavistic adventurous tendencies are only masked by civilized education, we were far from attributing any real significance to it.

Even so, a certain unease resulted from it, which gradually took possession of all of us: de Flers, so nervous, fell silent; Turny did not think of developing the amusing sophisms of his theory of flirtation, his favorite theme; d'Albas, who had emerged from the Barone d'Yssel's "five o'clock," had paused in spreading his gossip; Verbel was no longer sustaining the conversation about art that he had begun.

Ought we to attribute that imprecise hint of melancholy to the wintry day and the mists that were bring it to a close? Something of the dolorous disquiet of the dusk came in through the large bay windows, framed by dark curtains, in spite of the warm, comfortable, luxurious atmosphere. In the park, the snow was settling the soft caress of its flakes on the rough and leafless branches of the large trees. They fell slowly, swirling, tinted pink by the occidental blaze, with the result that the sky, vaguely darkened, sometimes reddened by the flight of the sun, seemed to be dropping the bloody down-feathers of wounded swans, whose crimson agony was extended through infinite space.

But the point at which our communal, albeit unacknowledged, embarrassment, sharpened to an almost brutal sensation, was when the prince, who was accustomed to listen in a taciturn manner to the buzz of conversations that were alternately grave and futile, cheerful and sincere, began to speak, while leaning his elbow on the precious dresser. Ordinarily, as if enclosed in the constant privacy of his own thoughts, he liked to permit his companions to say what was on their minds, without his impassivity testifying to any satisfaction or boredom, apparently preferring, in such assaults, the role of spectator to that of combatant, in spite of it being generally assumed that he wielded a fine blade. What pressing reason, then, drove him to emerge from his reserve? He was doubtless influenced by a serious motive, for his voice was slightly altered, and the native harshness of his accent reappeared, liberated by emotion.

"Have you ever wondered, Messieurs," he began, "what would became of a man who, after having traveled for a long time in the darkness of error, like the philosopher's prisoners chained in a cavern, and duped like them by the illusory silhouettes of deceptive shadows, suddenly found himself confronted by the dawn of truth, admitted to the contemplation of a hitherto-unsuspected reality? What sentiments might he experience? Even if your minds have never asked such questions, if I begged you to reply to them anyway, you would think it perfectly natural, would you not, that the liberation is question ought to bring with it, for the captive, a joy, a delight, rendered more than comprehensible by his victory over doubt and ignorance?

"Well, that man's situation is mine. Now, from the revelation granted to me, only a few hours separate us, and you see me now, plunged since then in the worst kind of anguish. You would have guessed wrongly in concluding that the knowledge would be joyful. I know now, and I would certainly prefer not to know."

That unusual speech, in combination with the agitation that had not escaped us, testified to a kind of expansive impulsiveness, evident characteristic of the alarm admitted by Ourousoff. We were undoubtedly witnessing the result of a mental struggle in which the patient and mute stoicism to which the prince had accustomed us had just been vanquished.

"During a sojourn in Genoa fifteen yeas ago," he continued, "a banal motive led me to the palace of the Marquise de C***. It was a matter, so far as I can remember, of some charitable project. Special circumstances, which you shall discover, have inscribed the exact date in my memory, with was the tenth of November. It was almost dark when I was introduced into Madame de C***'s drawing room, and I was waiting indifferently for her arrival when my gaze was suddenly attracted by a portrait decorating one of the panels of the room.

"The picture, painted in oils and of rather large dimensions, represented a masculine individual of a natural grandeur. The work itself had nothing remarkable about it, and was signed by an unknown name. What captured my attention, therefore, was a singular disposition: crowning long ornamental candlesticks, two rigid white candles stood up vertically, with small luminous feathery flames at the summit, unaffected by any draught; a rain of reflections splashed the forged iron chimeras of the supports and the plinths of the ledge with bright orange, and set sparkling darts in the frame; and the portrait, bathed in their warmth, took on changing aspects under the caress of that light, which seemed to animate it.

"My conversation with the Marquise lasted a few minutes, in the course of which, as you can easily imagine, I carefully refrained from asking any indiscreet question, even though I already felt a keen curiosity welling up within me. I soon learned from a mutual friend that the portrait was that of the Marquis de C***. I also knew that Madame de C***'s marriage had been the conclusion of a love affair that had impassioned all of Genoa at the time. A more-than-sentimental affection that followed the concluded union had, it was said, had irreparable effects on the Marquis' reason.

"In spite of this information, the strangeness of the inexplicable religious reverence I had remarked in the palace—which, in itself, was none of my concern—affected me in a singular fashion. I felt haunted by a kind of need to know more about the reason for that devotion.

"I ought to confess—it will perhaps assist you to understand the extraordinary intensity of that absurd possession—that I had previously been subjected, involuntarily, to certain reminiscences that had imposed themselves upon me with the same force.

Thus, on beginning to think about some insignificant object, the exact name of which in my mother tongue did not immediately come to mind, I was sometimes overwhelmed by an excessive desire, which was far from being justified by its trivial objective, to recover the term that had escaped me. I seemed then no longer to be myself—or, to put it better, that a part of myself was lacking. So, I could not rest until the moment when, either spontaneously or by some mnemonic artifice, the memory came back to me.

"Now, in the circumstance I'm recalling, the same anxious state of mind had overtaken me, this time with a more concrete objective, but one more difficult of satisfaction. What was the significance of those candles illuminating the portrait of the Marquis de C***? Suffering horribly from the anguishing research, extremely irritated by an emotion that was almost painful, I thought I was going mad. All of my mental faculties were despotically enslaved by that idea, which took over my mind imperiously and left no room, in its powerful jealousy, for any other speculation, even though my reason strove to demonstrate to me the absurdity of wanting to know the solution to the enigma.

"I was glad when, at length, that persecution eased of its own accord, having almost convinced me, in order to put a end to it, and in defiance of all convention, to go to the Palazzo C***, whatever the cost, to obtain the explanation for which I was so avid from the Marquise."

The prince paused momentarily in his unexpected confession. We remained silent, and that silence dressed the customary décor of our conversations with a solemn appearance. As the night had darkened, we could no longer see the snow falling outside. In the large room, the lamps shed a softer light, which lent objects, and even people, a dreamlike aspect.

Again, Ourousoff's voice rose up. "One encounters extraordinary combinations in life: coincidences created by the concurrence of disparate events perhaps demonstrating the intervention of a power superior to chance—for the success of a mosaic of circumstances, framed with such precision that a finished design results therefrom, seems so improbable without a directive power, that its plausibility retreats before the necessary effort. Furthermore, the unknown with which any attempt of that sort subsequently collides, renders the realization impossible.

"Be that as it may, one sometimes witnesses that realization of unforeseen ends, which occur independently of any voluntary determination or any plan conceived in advance, seemingly at the instigation of some kind of unidentifiable power. Thus, it was given to me to get to the bottom of the mystery that I had sensed during my visit to the Palazzo C***. Indeed, I met the Marquis himself, two years after my departure from Italy, when the first incident, which had affected me so much, was already effaced from my memory.

"I was dining at the home of Dr. Dalenoff, one of my old schoolfellows, who is a knowledgeable alienist and the director of a sanitarium in Momonowa-Datcha. Dalenoff had the habit of admitting to his table the most docile and least afflicted of his patients; he did not depart from the custom for a former comrade like myself.

"In the course of the evening, a young woman began to play on the piano, with a real artistic flair, Beethoven's Pastoral Symphony. Are you, like me, sensitive to the penetrating charm of that music? It has never left me indifferent; I have never been able to hear it without being moved. So, as soon as the marvelous pianist had reached the conclusion of the andante, I was gripped by the need for expansion that invites us, in order to savor our impressions more fully, to share then with others; and, perceiving someone who was not unknown to me close by, I began speaking to him.

"'Forgive me,' I said, 'did I not meet you the other day, with the doctor, in Moscow, near the Kalouga gate?"

"'You're undoubtedly mistaken,' he replied, mildly, 'for on the tenth of November it will be eight years since I have left this place. But my name will perhaps assist one of us to obtain more precise information from our memory. I'm the Marquis de C***.'

"The first measures of the adagio were resounding; we were obliged to restrict ourselves to that brief introduction. At first, the name that my interlocutor had given me had not struck a chord, but then I realized the reason for my error. The tenth of November, in Genoa, the candles, the picture, the Marquise—my former obsession! All of that past suddenly flooded forth, tumultuously, inundating my soul with disturbance; and when it died down, retreating gradually, it was to leave behind an alluvial deposit of confused thoughts. In that terrain, fertile for such seeds, because it was confused of the debris of the past, where so many others had germinated, a desire soon rose up, with imperious rapidity, in the fashion of those of yesteryear. An increasing impatience filled me with anguish, to talk to the Marquis in order to discover his story…and that idea soon dominated me to the point of making me yearn for an immediate end to the admirable melody, to which, in any other circumstances I would have listened gratefully, almost with ecstasy.

"When I was alone with the Marquis, in a billiard-room abandoned by players who had been attracted by the music, the latter looked at me for a long time; then an ionic crease hollowed out two bitter furrows in his face, and curled his lip.

"'You were probably surprised to find me here, and you want to ask me the reason for my residence in this country, far from my own!'

"When I acquiesced with a nod of the head, he went on: 'First of all, with your consent, I would like to ask you a few necessary questions, for the continuation of this conversation will depend on your answers. I would like, above all, to know whether your mind is determinedly cloistered in a confirmed skepticism, remaining suspicious of anything that surpasses the known and immediate truth, refusing to admit that which the present sum of its acquisitions drives it to condemn to the oblivion of false or baseless conceptions?

"'No, you say? In that case you admit that phenomena present themselves to which admitted laws and banal formulas are not applicable? You would not have the scornful smile of false scholars before a case that surprises them; you would believe, if you observed it, in its existence, and would not deny it for theoretical reasons? Then place your hand, please, upon my breast, there...do you feel the heart palpitating in is usual place? You don't perceive *anything*, do you? *You should not perceive anything!*'

"In truth, Messieurs, I assure you; *I could not feel any heartbeat.*

"'Will you believe me now,' said the Marquis, passionately, 'will you believe me, in defiance of all the implausibility that such an affirmation assumes—will you believe me? Well, my heart is no longer there— you have observed that—and it is the Marquise who has *stolen my heart!*'

"He had pronounced those last words with a force, and a heart-rending tone, that had shaken my being profoundly, reawakening there by means of the supernatural an ancient mystic soul dormant in mine—but it was only after a long interval of reflection and anxiety that an idea sprang forth in my brain with the force, as it was born, almost of an intuition: *What if the Marquis were telling the truth?*

"Oh, all the arguments that you might evoke in

such a case, I summoned, in order to reject that exotic hypothesis. To steal the heart from an individual's breast! Is it not illogical, inconceivable, in contradiction with all our knowledge, and the facts themselves, to suppose that such a bizarre story might be possible?

"Afterwards, I began insensibly to think that certain scientific discoveries, recognized in our day, were opposed and rejected before being universally admitted. Might the problem be susceptible of such a solution? The alternatives of skepticism and faith seriously occupied my brain, where a leaven of hope remained to me that nothing seemed to justify.

"Behold, nevertheless, the marvelous organization of the fatality that I mentioned just now. A few weeks ago, the Palazzo C*** was sold, following the death of the Marquise. I went to Genoa, having learned about it, and made the acquisition of various objects. Among them was a box, which I received yesterday.

"This morning, I opened it, out of a perfectly natural curiosity, and do you know what it contained? Neither you, Turny, nor you, d'Albas, not any of you, in truth… no, none of you could guess what the box contained… what it still contains.…"

The prince had pronounced these words in a hoarse voice, which summoned a frisson, and his eyes were ablaze when he opened, tremulously, one of the panels of the Renaissance dresser on which he had been leaning during his narration.

He brought out a box.

We had drawn closer together, all of us having

experienced, in spite of being skeptical, the little thrill of terror that the assault of the unknown procures, for when the lid was raised, with the dry click of a depressed catch, an instinctive movement of recoil was produced in the group.

On the faded white satin, more yellow than ivory, sat one of those rather commonplace items of jewelry, a little heart in enameled gold, which was shining feebly.

No one, however, sketched a smile. His face disfigured, Ourousoff cried, with the haggard gestures of a somnambulist living a nightmare: "Look, look at that heart! Look at it, red, moist, swollen with blood! See how it is palpitating and suffering for being separated from its master! Ha! Do you believe now, do you believe in *the stolen heart!*"

The logs in the fireplace had just completed their extinction, tinting the beautiful caryatids of the fireplace with pale carmine.

Everyone's face darkened, and, as if the wind of madness, instantaneously unchained, constrained us to bend over, our beads bowed. That was because the fear was rising within us of being subject in our turn, without any hope of defense, to the distress of terror, and to the mysterious hallucination whose emprise had possessed our friend.

THE CINQ-BRAS

We were in the second line, where we were actively engaged in digging trenches, shelters and tunnels on the plateau of R***, in case of a retreat. A few kilometers ahead of us, the battle was continuing, only discernible by means of the noise and the smoke, for we could not see any cannons, or human beings. The battery emplacements, the lines and the enemy were only revealed to us by the fire of the 75s and the big guns, and the shell-bursts. In the rare moments of silence, large flocks of crows passed overhead, beneath the low winter sky.

That morning, half an hour before the resumption of the work, I had gone into the wood on my own, in advance of the detail of which I was a part. Although it was nearly noon, it was one of those days that seem like a long twilight; the clouds and the mists remain tinted by the colors of evening. In the clearing, the fire we were feeding with the debris of our construction was burning high and bright. Nearby, on a rustic bench, our work-party, sheltered from the wind by a hurdle set on its end, a sergeant—the supervisor of our endeavors—was sitting. I saluted him. With an affable gesture, he indicated a place beside him.

Once before, I had found him alone in that place, and the exceedingly severe NCO that he was in the service had been transformed into an amiable and cultivated companion. I had learned then that he had commenced rather pressurized studies, with a view to a career in the liberal arts, which had been abruptly interrupted, and that since then, married, the young father of a family, and sent into the civil service, he had retained a kind of nostalgia, so to speak, for literature, and especially for philosophy. That is why I was not surprised to see him sad and pensive. He was often absorbed in the contemplation of the play of flames, which, like that of the sea, can be watched almost indefinitely without lassitude. I therefore attributed his melancholy attitude and the isolation in which I had caught him to a combination the depressing effects of the sunless day and the sentiment of regret I have just mentioned, which sometimes darkened his mood.

We remained silent for a few minutes. He was mechanically polishing a cane with a handful of dry leaves, and I was respecting his reverie when, abruptly turning his fine head toward me, with his regular features, striped by a thin black moustache, and his brown eyes, shinier than usual, he said to me: "Forget my stripes for a moment. Only see before you a man, and a man who's suffering, suffering terribly. I hesitated for a long time before speaking to you, but I believe you're the only person here in whom I can confide, who might perhaps understand. Personally, I don't know any more. I've tried, I can assure you, but no, I can't! There are times, you know, when I don't want ever to go back."

"What about your wife and your son?"

"Them! It would be better for them if...." He did not finish his sentence; a despairing gesture completed it, which rendered it more tragic than the sound of the cannonade.

"Come on, Sergeant!" I said. "It's winter now, but spring will come again, the sun, and victory, and peace...and you'll forget...."

He interrupted me. "I'll never forget!"

"What! A moment of discouragement is quickly past. One fights!"

"One fights against discouragement. One fights against a fit of the blues. Oh, if you knew what I had to fight, and how much energy I've expended in that struggle...I've expended so much, my friend, that I no longer have any left, and now I'm hesitating. After all, who can assure me that, when you've heard me out, you'll be any more indulgent to me than I am?"

I thought he had suddenly gone mad, for, abruptly getting to his feet, he had pronounced that final sentence in a wild and bitter tone.

He sighed deeply, sat down again, avoided looking me in the face, and went on, more calmly: "Whatever you might think of me, afterwards, promise that you'll give me your verdict, frankly...."

"Sergeant, what I know about you...."

"You don't know anything! Even I, I repeat, no

longer know anything!"

"Well, I promise you I'll be sincere."

"Thanks! I'm tranquilized, as you see. I sense that I'll have the courage to speak and…it's better that I speak. Do you remember the Cinq-Bras?"

"Of course."

Immediately, I saw once again that September morning, when we had arrived at the intersection of roads that gave its name to the former farm, transformed into a hunting-lodge and flanked by a little inn. From the intersection of the two main roads, which cut across one another at right-angles, departed the fifth arm, a poor earthen track that went down to a spring and then climbed up a hill, behind the crest of which our artillerymen were already hollowing out the emplacements for a battery. Our company had stopped there, and had rapidly crenellated the walls of the farm and had dug horse-trenches along the main road. All day long the troops had been filing past, going forward to where the cannon-fire could be heard, and then, at irregular intervals, the rhythmic sound of machine-guns and the crackle of rifle-fire.

Toward evening, the automobiles going to look for and bring back the wounded began to go by. The innkeeper, a tall man with an unhealthy and worried expression, thin and bent, had remained constantly sitting on a stone bench in front of the door, leaving his wife, a cheerful pretty blonde, to serve us.

"He needs air," the wife had said.

Their cellar was admirably provisioned. It was very

warm. When night fell—a very dark, moonless night—many of the men were in high spirits, a few completely drunk, including some of those in the section on guard duty. As that wasn't mine, I went to bed in the barn, fairly early. Tired out, I had fallen sleep rapidly, and only retained a vague memory of an incident that had occurred in the middle of the night.

A confused sound of voices had woken me up—the thick and heavy voice of a drunken man and the clear and mordant voice of an officer. It came from the room transformed into a guard-post beside which I was lying. A ray of yellow light filtered under the door. Then the roar of engines had prevented me from hearing any more. The cold glare of headlights pierced the high windows of the barn, illuminating the bodies lying in the straw. Before the convoy had finished passing by, I had gone back to sleep.

The next day, I found out that a drunken sentinel had not challenged a lieutenant who was making his round; he had claimed that it was not the drink that was responsible for his failure, but rather than his attention had been attracted by signals that he had seen at a window. The excuse had been deemed false, the window being that of a room in which an NCO was sleeping.

As I reminded the sergeant of all that—he listened to me without moving, his eyes fixed on the burning wood of the fire—an abrupt emotion overwhelmed me. Wasn't the man sitting beside me the one in the room at the Cinq-Bras? His reticence, the language that I had been near to considering extravagant, his melancholy, his depressed attitude—that ensemble of meager facts suddenly acquired a brutal force that imposed a conviction upon me: that the sentinel might have been right.

I endured a frightful moment then. A bitter wave of shame submerged me, as if I had been the guilty party myself. How could an NCO in my company have lowered himself to that?

In spite of the care I took to hide it, my disturbance was so evident that he noticed it and said, sadly, as if he had read my thought: "Yes, it was me that was sleeping in the room at the Cinq-Bras. Should I go on?"

I had almost wanted him to deny it immediately. I was torn between disgust and anger, at the same time as a puerile desire to weep twisted my mouth and burned my eyelids. I made a violent effort to constrain myself to reply: "Yes! Go on! Speak, I beg you!"

My somber voice had informed him as to my sentiments. He smiled, timidly, and yet ironically. "Oh," he said, "unfortunately, it's not as simple as that...I mean, what you've doubtless been able to think. I don't hold it against you, anyway...you promised me you'd be sincere...I'd almost rather it had been that, for that would have been finished long ago, and I'd have suffered less. It's precisely because I don't know whether I have the right, for the sake of my wife and child, simply to stick my head over a parapet once and for all, that I've struggled so much and I torture myself every day...."

The hope returned to me that he had only been capable of a brief lapse, since redeemed, by his repentance and by more positive actions. Scarcely had those hasty deductions been formulated in my mind, however, already accompanied by a sort of sentimental relief, a soothing of my first impression, than he continued.

"You've doubtless not forgotten that low room in the Cinq-Bras inn: the window screened by a blanket in order to prevent the light being seen from outside; the long table cluttered with glasses and sticky with spilled liquids; the husband sitting, like some sinister bird of prey, in a wicker armchair next to an extinct stove covered with empty bottles; the wife—very blonde, very cheerful—responding to everything by laughing, and often accepting a drink. You, I know, left early with your comrades. I stayed, in company with two colleagues, big Thiriot, and Hettel, the Alsatian, who was on guard. He soon left us to go and rejoin his men.

Thiriot amused himself by getting us drunk— the woman and me. I didn't really notice. Gradually, however, things and people were surrounded with mist, appearing to me as in a dream. I became chatty—me, the silent one—and said things whose boldness astonished me, or seeming excessively amusing…me, who hardly ever laughs. Two things, however, remain clear in my memory.

"The first is the attitude, like a fearful animal, that the woman sometimes had as she passed close to her husband. He darted harsh looks at her then, the master; she looked at him with the expression of submission that some beaten dogs have....

"The second was my astonishment on seeing that man get up and speak. Until then, he'd seemed to me to be some item of furniture, strangely animated but nevertheless incapable of separating himself from the armchair he occupied. It's probable, too, that drunkenness augmented my surprise.

"He explained to us that the owners of the hunting-lodge had confided to him not only the keys to the house and the farm but the surveillance of their woods, and that the war didn't prevent the old poachers who had stayed in the next village from setting their snares. He therefore prepared to make a round in order to try to catch one, and asked big Thiriot to go with him in order to inform Hettel and his sentinels.

I tried to get up to go out with them, but the alcohol was weighing me down terribly, and I fell back, while the door closed.

The woman laughed loudly. "'Come on!' she said. 'You'll never be able to get to your room on your own. I'll take you.'

"After that, nothing subsists in my memory but fragments of sensations, poorly-connected shreds of images. How did I get out of that room, climb the stairs, go along the corridor between the inn and the hunting lodge, lie down and then go to sleep? I can't remember any of that—nothing precise.

"I was woken up be a sharp pain.

"The headlights of autos traveling in convoy on the road threw intermittent lights into the room where I was. I saw the innkeeper's wife, half naked, curled up beside me. Her loose blonde hair fell over her face, still reddened by drunkenness. She squeezed my arm convulsively, digging her nails into my flesh. I was so confused that I couldn't make a movement or say a word.

"'Listen,' she said. 'My husband!'

"I did, indeed, hear him outside, responding to the call of a sentinel.

"'If he finds me here, he'll kill me…oh, don't move.…'

"With incredible rapidity, she leapt out of the bed, picked up her scattered clothing, which she stuffed into a cupboard, then came back to slip under the covers into the space between the mattress and the wall.

"Mechanically, I rearranged the pillows and sheets myself. Then I closed my eyes. A damp hand sought mine and clung on to it. Long minutes went by. Finally, a heavy tread resounded on the stairway, went along the corridor and paused briefly before arriving at our door.

"The man knocked. 'Sergeant X***?' he asked.

"Thiriot's voice replied: 'He's well away.'

"Almost immediately, discreet knocks resonated.

"I wouldn't have been capable of speaking without giving myself away, so intense was my emotion. The woman's hand clenched harder, gripping mine like a drowning man clutching at a branch.

"The man came in.

"My heart was pounding in my breast, like that of a

cornered animal. There was a ringing in my ears, and in my turn, I squeezed the small hand that was holding mine with all my might, in order not to tremble wretchedly.

"'Sergeant…!' But he lowered the tone almost immediately as he came nearer, while continuing the sentence he'd begun. 'I've brought your torch—the electric torch you left downstairs.'

"He shut up, and very slowly and softly, as if talking to himself, he went on: 'It's obvious that he's not used to drinking…poor bugger! He might be killed tomorrow…best let him sleep.'

"That unexpected pity caused me real distress, and the man's presence became unbearable to me. I'd have preferred an odious brutality, or at least indifference. Red gleams lit up behind my eyelids, which I attributed to my anger. Later, I wonder whether they might not have come from auto reflectors, or from my torch, whose switch he was maneuvering.…

"He went out. His footsteps drew away.

"Slowly, moving like a she-cat, the woman emerged, and, before I was able to stop her, crushed my lips with a kiss. Suddenly, in spite of the roar of the autos, which were still filing past, we made out the sound of an altercation. The woman hid again. I listened.

"Now the voices were coming from below, from the guard-post. 'You didn't see me coming because you weren't doing your duty, and you were distracted from your duty because you're drunk. That's shameful. I won't punish you as much as you deserve: you're a reservist and the father of a family; but if this happens again....'

"'Thank you, Lieutenant. It's true that I've had a drink. I've been drinking, that's true, I won't hide it—but I'm not drunk enough not to do my duty, or the Sergeant would have stood me down already. If I didn't see you, Lieutenant, it's because I was watching that window I showed you, where someone was making signals.'

"'You should have been watching the road. Anyway, you must have seen the reflection of headlights on the panes, since your sergeant's told you that it's the room of one of his colleagues.'

"'Possibly, Lieutenant, but I'm not drunk! I've had a drink but I'm not drunk, and what I saw, I saw! Thank you, Lieutenant, for what you said just now, but even though I ought to go to prison, or worse, I can't say that I didn't see what I saw. There were red lights, with gaps. It was definitely signals. Perhaps the sergeant isn't sleeping in that room?'

"'We'll go and see.'

"You can guess the rest: the lieutenant's visit, my interrogation. Could I tell him the truth, with that woman beside me?

"Now, as you'll remember, the next day, the village of N*** was destroyed, the battery-emplacement on the dirt road located and copiously deluged....

"Yes of course, it's possible that there's no connection. I've told myself that. Simple coincidence! As for the lights the sentinel had seen, they might have been produced by the innkeeper idly playing with the switch of my torch. Then again, if he had been a spy, his nocturnal excursion would have given him enough time to go through the lines and communicate with the enemy. He had the password to get back.

"I've told myself all that. Except that, in spite of everything, I can't get the idea out of my head that, that night, at the Cinq-Bras, it was an atrocious comedy that that woman and that man played, making me their accomplice! And most of all, I think that I'll never know the truth...."

The sergeant had hidden his face in his hands.

What should I have said in reply?

At that moment, groups of men came into the clearing. It was time to start work again, and I had to rejoin them.

The next day, orders arrived in the night and we had to leave the plateau of R***. Afterwards, I didn't have any opportunity to keep my promise, because the dictates of fate kept me away from Sergeant X***.

THE EVOLUTION
OF LITERATURE

One of the most significant characteristics of the great laws of Evolution, such as they emerge from the works of biologists and philosophers, is that they do not apply solely to one of the genres of manifestation of general activity, but to all of its modes. And from that viewpoint, the triple parallelism invoked by Haeckel between the ontogenic, phylogenic and paleontogenic series is susceptible, as Romanes has demonstrated, of being extended even to the development of thought.[8]

Without, however, going so far, and limiting ourselves to the particular point of view with which we are concerned here, it is easy to render account of the fact that evolution of the literary genre is intimately association with Evolution as a whole, to which it is important to attach it, if one wishes to possess a conductive thread, a sure guide to steer through the complexities that presently embarrass questions of

---

8. George Romanes (1848-1894) was a friend of Charles Darwin and Thomas Henry Huxley who attempted to use the theory of natural selection to lay the foundations of what he called "comparative psychology," following lines of thought that Darwin also attempted to develop in *The Expression of the Emotions in Man and Animals* (1872).

literature, or, to put it better, a solid basis of appreciation in matters concerning productions of that order.

In order not to stray from contemporary observation, it appears that the multiple methods that succeeded Romanticism can be rationally arranged under the unique heading of Naturalism.

It does not astonish us to see attached to the same school in this fashion realism, verism[9] and the analytical novel. That is because, in this sense, the neorealists, the naturalists and the psychologists represent the varieties of the same phase of the evolutionary development marked in the stage of the progress of our mind by the advent of the doctrine of positivism, represented in France by August Comte and his disciples. That theory, extolling the observation of facts as the immediate source of all knowledge, demonstrating the inanity of hypotheses and deductions based on purely ideal conceptions, not only influenced scientists, but litterateurs, who—which will only seem surprising at first glance—have an incontestable solidarity with all the other laborers of human thought. In consequence, fiction is no longer adopted as the sole artistic ideal and there is a preoccupation with the discovery of tangible foundations, on which the new edifice is based.

That has given rise to the modern novelists, and it

---

9. The term *verisme* [verism] was used occasionally in late nineteenth-century literary criticism but swiftly became obsolete; it was borrowed from Classical studies, where it referred to a late period in Roman art when statues were produced that were not idealized but reproduced all the imperfections to which human faces and bodies are subject. In modern English parlance, the philosophy of representation is usually summarized by the phrase "warts and all."

is permissible in that regard to identify the naturalists with the psychologists, for—has not Paul Bourget recently said as much?—the divergences that separate them are only apparent and quite superficial. Both give evidence, in fact, of the same preoccupation, a similar concern to take constant inspiration from the simple data of nature. The former, it is true, describe the external, objective face and the latter the internal, subjective face of the phenomena of life. On the other hand, while the naturalists ordinary choose working people as protagonists, noting their phenomenology in their own element of action, the psychologists prefer, for their part, the study of individuals higher in the social scale, whose more intellectual occupations are more conducive to the study of their states of mind. It can nevertheless be seen that these are not essential differences, for, in sum, the object and the method are fundamentally identical. The authors of both groups are guided by a similar desire to synthesize realities, which itself distinguishes their intimate nature.

There is another no less important consequences of the laws of Evolution whose application it is appropriate to grasp here: that which is known as *differentiation*, or, to put it another way, the progressive tendency that, in normal individuals, makes use of increasingly specialized and improved organs of increasingly delicate function. That tendency is also found, under the name of the law of the division of labor, in the various stages of the progress of industry. As for the domain under discussion, it does not escape the rule, and it is one of the merits of the late Guyau[10] to have established the demonstration of the fact from that viewpoint.

That is what is fearlessly ventured, by a sort of reaction against naturalism, which is exaggerated in the direction of idealism, by decadents, symbolists, romantics, and so on. They constitute, in this sense, products of literary "degeneration," by comparison with what that term implies for pathologists, their common characteristic residing in an abnormal recall of ancestral forms presently disappeared. Writings of this sort can be seen as representative, in the literary order, of that which is represented, in the physical order by monsters subjected to an arrested development; and, to perfect the parallel, is not the undeniable movement of curiosity that they have provoked analogous in all points to that produced by teratological exhibitions? There is, therefore, a genuine retrograde movement here, a kind of atavistic regression.

To return to the two essential modalities of the novel, the novel of analysis is perhaps already considered as a differentiated equivalent of the naturalist novel, which, moreover, it has succeeded. Now, in works of this sort, such as they have been revealed at present, one cannot fail to remark that the psychological formula by which they are inspired has remained that of the "spiritualist" school of yesteryear, of which Professor Ribot once said: "Although it is still fairly popular, the old

10. The philosopher and poet Jean-Marie Guyau (1854-1888) attempted a fusion of classical Epicureanism with modern Utilitarianism; he developed the concept of anomie taken over by, and nowadays associated with, Émile Durkheim

psychology is doomed."

So, departing from the principle posed by the same author, to wit, that "the psychologist must renounce metaphysics and the metaphysician psychology" we believe that, similarly, in the novel, one ought to take account of the new doctrines, by accepting "a psychology without the soul"—which is to say, one based in the biological sciences—and not forgetting that "every psychic state is invariably associated with a nervous state."

For our part, we have contrived to arrive at the expression of this new degree of differentiation. We have considered, in the first place, with the naturalists, that the endeavors of art should only be inspired by objective observations; secondly, with the analysts, that, progress having abused, in a sense, the exterior, gross and easily observable aspects of things, literary endeavor ought to be pursued in the direction of internal observation; and finally that, psychology having now emerged from the purely spiritualist phase in which it was previously confined, isolating itself from the other branches of science, these attempts ought to be brought into accord with the evolution that places psychological phenomena definitively on known terrain. In brief, it is from the data of experimental psychology that we are departing.

In the same way that the naturalists, in the preparatory period of their works, began with an in-depth examination of what they called "the documents," we have subsequently devoted ourselves to researching the bases of experimentation before utilizing them for literary adaptation. Thus, we have restricted ourselves in the first place to studying, almost scientifically, certain subjects whose gross mental deformations, permitting the notation of more appreciable coexistent physical variations, ought to facilitate the analysis of simple modalities of states of consciousness and their physical concomitants.[11] It has thus been given to us to present in literary form, in a series of essays published by the *Mercure de France* under the title "Contes de l'Au-Delà," in which the stages of this development are clearly marked, the cases emerging from mental pathology.

In this novel, we have attempted the employment of this new procedure and, if one might put it that way, its practical demonstration. It is, in fact, a matter here of a study of Love—a study of which we have composed the technical part in another work.[12] The general method of knowledge consisting, in accordance with to the definition of P. Blocq and Onanoff, of the identification of determined attributes of things with the mental

---

11. Author's note: "I cannot thank too much, in this regard, Dr. Séglas, a physician at the Salpêtrière, who, with Dr. Paul Blocq, has been my initiator in these matters. I also address the homage of a sincere gratitude to the memory of the late Dr. J. Onanoff, in whom science has just lost one of her best and most zealous servants." The references are to Charcot's one-time assistant Jules Séglas (1856-1939), who made a detailed study of delusions and hallucinations, the influence of which extended (and still extends) far beyond Danville's work, and Jacques Onanoff (1860-1892), who wrote a book in collaboration with Paul Blocq on the symptomatology of nervous disorders.

12. Author's note: "'L'Amour est-il an état pathologique?' (To appear imminently in the *Revue philosophique*.)"

representations to which those same things have given rise, we have considered that Love can only represent a particular case of that law.

The origin of passion resides, in this way of seeing, in the fact of the identification of attributes of the beloved object with the mental representations that the subject has formed of an ideal lover (the identification is necessary to the consciousness). Every normal human being is, in consequence, unconsciously amorous, and will only become consciously—which is to say, really—amorous in the case that the procedure of identification takes place within him. That mechanism does not function in cases of psychic disequilibrium; it might, for example, result in the "inability to love," such as it has been formulated by Paul Bourget, but in the subjective mode.

If I have attempted, on the threshold of this first book, to uncover the inductions preliminary to its formation, to show the source of inspiration on which it draws, and to explain the reasons for being that appear to justify it, I will doubtless be excused when I admit that, far from trying to swell this modest work to the amplitude of the general views that I have just expounded, my goal was rather, and more legitimately—in the eyes of those who might take an interest in it—to try something new, and to indicate to those who are confused by the number of literary schools, the most logical direction in which they might be able to orientate themselves.

Paris, 1 November 1892

ABOUT THE TRANSLATOR

BRIAN STABLEFORD has translated more than a hundred volumes of French prose into English. His principal interests are the French Romantic Movement and its Decadent/Symbolist aftermath, with particular reference to the evolution of the *conte cruel*, and the evolution of the *roman scientifique* from its origins in the eighteen-century *conte philosophique* to the aftermath of the Great War of 1914-18.

www.ingramcontent.com/pod-product-compliance
Lightning Source LLC
Chambersburg PA
CBHW031425250626
47155CB00004B/1625